Gaia had despised Tatiana for every one of her offensive assumptions and lofty judgments. And they had all been correct. All Tatiana's holier-than-thou, high-and-mighty presumptions had been disgustingly, embarrassingly right on the money. Bringing this low-level hustler into the house had been a terrible mistake. Terrible mistake—there was the understatement of the century.

Gaia's lousy judgment and reverse snobbery were about to get them both killed.

Don't miss any books in this thrilling new series from Pocket Books:

FEARLESS™

All Pocket Book titles are available by post from:
**Simon & Schuster Cash Sales, P.O. Box 29,
Douglas, Isle of Man IM99 1BQ**
Credit cards accepted. Please telephone 01624 836000,
Fax 01624 670923, Internet http://www.bookpost.co.uk
or email: bookshop@enterprise.net for details

FEARLESS™

FRANCINE PASCAL

HURT

POCKET
BOOKS

To Avery Glize-Kane

An imprint of Simon & Schuster UK Ltd
A Viacom Company
Africa House, 64-78 Kingsway, London WC2B 6AH

Produced by 17th Street Productions, Inc.
A division of Daniel Weiss Associates, Inc.
33 West 17th Street, New York, NY 10011

A CIP catalogue record for this book is
available from the British Library

ISBN 07434 40544

1 3 5 7 9 10 8 6 4 2

Printed and bound in Great Britain by Omnia Books Ltd, Glasgow

Have you ever looked in the mirror and started to wonder if the real you was the one in the mirror and you were actually the mirror image?

Or what about this—have you ever woken up from a dream and realized that you were actually still dreaming, and then kind of lost track for a while of what was reality and what was the dream?

No, I'm not high. I know that's what you're thinking already, but the fact is, I don't do drugs. I just think too much.

Okay, here's my point. Whether you've read the works of Plato or you've just warbled a couple of rounds of "Row, Row, Row Your Boat" in the backseat of a car, you've still come across this theory: Life is but a dream. Rings a bell, yes?

Well, I have to say, I think that pretty succinctly describes my life at this point. After everything I've been through and

GAIA

discovered in the last forty-eight hours or so, I'm honestly not sure I can tell the difference between reality and dreams. Nor am I sure I want to. Yes, sir, I am so deep through the looking glass at this point, I may just have to change my name to Alice.

Example: My uncle has informed me that I wasn't born fearless. He says my fear genes are totally intact and that in fact I've only been fearless because of some kind of serum that my father and the Agency injected into my bloodstream when I was a baby.

Follow me on this one.

So my uncle gives me this new injection. This serum that's supposed to *counter* what my father did to me and make me feel fear again. ("Drink me." "Eat me." Are you with me on *this?*) And once I took the serum, let's just say, for the sake of brevity, that I went nuts. Real nuts.

Yeah. . . there were delusions, paranoid freak-outs, the works. But after a few revelations,

the most important of which was
that Loki has created at least
two Josh clones (yes, clones—welcome to my dream world), I think
I've finally recovered from my
very unfortunate experiment with
fear.

   But here's the thing. I honestly don't know if my uncle was
lying or not. So which thing is
real? Am I fearless, and I was
just temporarily dreaming I could
feel fear? Or am I actually capable of fear, and I've just been
living a seventeen-year dream
that I was fearless? I honestly
do not have a clue.

   Here's a much more immediate
example: Around four-thirty this
morning, I realized something
that I think I already knew. I am
in love with Ed Fargo. Not a temporary crush. Not any kind of
teenage puppy love or romantic
experimentation. Just love. Pure
and simple.

   But after the last forty-eight
hours of madness, I can't help
wondering. . . .

What is the reality and what is the dream? Have I, unbeknownst to myself, been in love with Ed for the last year and only dreaming we were nothing more than friends? Or are we still only friends in reality, and this glorious perfect morning is only a dream? See, I've fallen asleep and awoken so many times in the last forty-eight hours, I'm honestly not sure anymore. I've coasted in and out of sanity so many times, I'm not altogether sure I'm not insane at this very moment.

But if I am insane, or if lying next to Ed is only a dream, then I'm begging you, whoever makes these kinds of decisions up there, please, please don't let me wake up. Please just let me sleep. Because this dream is *so* superior to any reality I've had in months. And as long as everything around us stays quiet, I think perhaps it just might last.

His lips. . .
what was
it
about
his lips?

28

minutes

"DO YOU WANT ME TO CLOSE THE window?"

Ed had pulled his lips away from Gaia's and brought his head back just far enough to look her in the

Shivers

eyes. His hair was still hanging down on her forehead, keeping them connected, as he smiled at her with the most Ed-specific guileless adoration.

"Why?" Gaia whispered, doing her best to breathe regularly in spite of the fact that her heart was beating triplets.

"Aren't you freezing?" he whispered sweetly. "You're shivering like crazy."

Gaia froze from sheer embarrassment, though she wasn't the least bit cold. Her eyes froze over as well, with a momentary attack of deer-in-headlights syndrome. "Oh. . . y-yeah," she stammered. "The window. Good idea."

Ed reached over Gaia in the bed and dragged his bedroom window shut, cutting off what was left of the city street noise at five in the morning.

She actually would have much preferred to keep it open, but what was she supposed to say? Was she supposed to tell him the truth? That she was shivering from his kisses, and his soft lips on her neck, and the feeling of his palms and his fingertips running along her waist? That the shivering was some kind of involuntary physical manifestation of how inconceivably happy she was at this moment, on his bed, in his arms, in the abnormally bright mix of ocean blue moonlight and stark white New York streetlight?

No. That was unquestionably something to be felt and not to be said. Like a million other things she was feeling now, staring back into his eyes.

The brief window exchange had finally pulled their lips and bodies apart after twenty-eight minutes, and Ed leaned back to his pillow, running his finger along Gaia's cheek.

Just twenty-eight minutes. Gaia couldn't believe it. Twenty-eight minutes since she'd confessed—at least, in her own way—that she loved him. How could this version of them be only a half hour old?

But that really wasn't true, was it? Not if Gaia wanted to be completely honest with herself. Not if she wanted to dig past the paper-thin labels and relationship rules set up by the pre-*When Harry Met Sally* generation. The fact was, that movie wasn't just for liberal Upper West Side yuppie men and women over thirty. In truth, if all seventeen-year-olds could speak as honestly as Harry Burns and Sally Albright, then they, too, would have to confess that there was probably *something* else going on under their "best friendships" with members of the opposite sex.

"Friends" might once have been the label for Gaia and Ed, but given the particularly honest mood she was in at this moment, Gaia had to admit that in some

7

way, she and Ed had sort of been "courting" since the school year started. In spite of all the love and tragedies they'd experienced apart from each other. In spite of a million other things, Gaia and Ed were a constant.

Maybe that was why, once she'd admitted what she was feeling, it was suddenly so easy to be so close. Almost as if they'd been together this way the entire time. Twenty-eight minutes into this relationship, and Gaia was finding herself with a boyfriend whom she knew inside and out and trusted even more than she did herself.

Ed cocked his head and searched Gaia's eyes with a mildly bemused smile. "What are you thinking?"

"Nothing," Gaia responded instantly. Man, did she need to work on the spoken-honesty thing.

"You're still working on the spoken-honesty thing, aren't you?" Ed asked. God, he was good.

"No." Gaia squirmed. "I just. . ." *Oh, Gaia, cut it out. You've got nothing left to hide now.* "Yeah," she admitted. "Yeah, I'm having a little trouble in that category."

"Okay," Ed said purposefully, jamming his elbow into his pillow and leaning his head on his hand, "let's do a little exercise in spoken honesty—"

"Oh, hell, no," Gaia interrupted.

"Come on." Ed laughed. "It's five in the morning. Who's going to know? What, are you afraid?"

Oh, he didn't want to go there. Gaia didn't want go

there. That was the question of the hour. *The* question. Was her uncle's injection a phony or not? Was fear now a part of her life, or was that all a hoax? Was her fearlessness genetic or part of some governmental excuse for a science project put together by her father and a bunch of freakazoid CIA doctors? No, sir, she would not be going there. Not on this beautiful dark morning in this safe bed with her glorious new "everything" looking into her eyes. Whether she was now capable of fear or not, in this bed, with this boy, she wasn't afraid of anything.

"No," Gaia assured him. "I am most definitely not afraid."

"Fine, then you just have to answer a few questions honestly."

"Fine."

"Fine. Okay. Question one: Do you find me. . . *attractive?*"

"Okay, I quit," Gaia said, turning toward the window.

"Kidding," Ed laughed, pulling her back toward him.

"You've got one more shot," she said, with a comical glare.

"Okay," Ed agreed, staring into her eyes again. He shifted onto his stomach and moved closer until their noses were nearly touching. But he really shouldn't have done that. Not if the goal was to have a conversation. It had already been established in the last twenty-four hours that when the two of them got this close, talking was not the first inclination. "Okay. . . ," he began again. "All right. . ." Ed seemed unable to produce a full sentence since his eyes had refocused on Gaia's mouth. "Okay. . ."

His mouth was so close to hers, she could feel the consonants rolling off his lips. And the shivers had started again. First lightly in her toes. Then sudden heavy trembles in her stomach. His lips. . . what was it about his lips? Before she could answer her own question, she found that her hand had drifted up to his mouth to investigate. Without any specific orders from her brain, her fingers began to gently trace a line from his lips to the corner of his mouth.

"Um," he uttered, inching his face closer. "Do you. . . ?"

"What. . . ?" she whispered, doing her best to cover the shivers.

Ed seemed utterly dazed by her fingers. "Do you want—"

"Yes." Gaia pressed her lips against his, channeling all the pent-up energy of her trembling into her kiss. Ed responded with equal force, wrapping his hands tightly around her waist. But Gaia's T-shirt had ridden up slightly when he grabbed her, leaving Ed's wide palms suddenly pressed against her waist. This sent another bolt of electricity up her spine that in no way helped to calm her shivers.

Ed's shirt had also apparently hiked up slightly, and when Gaia's hands drifted down to his waist to hold him, her fingers ended up grazing the bottom of his exposed abs, sliding up along his muscular back, and clinging to his bare shoulders under his shirt. It might have been an accident, but it only led to higher-voltage trembling.

And with her lips on his lips and their hands clinging to each other's backs, Gaia slowly began to realize that the moment when her brain or her body would bring things to a halt did not seem to be coming. She didn't want to stop. There was no reason to stop. Not when she loved him this much. Not after building months of totally untainted trust. All she wanted now was to be closer to him. As close as was humanly possible.

Her hands on his bare back didn't have to be an accident. Not if she didn't want it to be. So she simply let her hands follow through. Without rushing or tugging, Gaia let her arms continue to slide upward, lifting Ed's T-shirt higher and higher off his chest, until he'd raised his arms and let her pull the T-shirt off.

She slid her hands across his bare shoulders and kissed him again as he returned his palms to the exposed small of her back. Now she could feel just how quickly his heart was beating.

But Ed pulled back momentarily, bringing his hands up to Gaia's face and giving her a kind but penetrating stare. "Gaia," he said between increasingly rapid breaths, "are we about to do what I think we're about to do?"

"I think so," she whispered breathlessly.

He kissed her again and then searched her eyes. "Are you sure you're ready?"

THE QUESTION WAS LIKE A LOUD,

piercing bell shaking Gaia awake from the floating dreamland of Ed's bed. All her warm tingles and electric vibrations took a sharp and very sudden turn. Her body continued to buzz, but it was as if all the sweetness and heat had been drained away, leaving a cold and constricting drone in its place.

Fade to Black

And there it was again. A feeling she'd honestly thought—well, at least *hoped*—she'd shaken for good. That dreadful, horrid, and unmercifully *yucky* sensation that Gaia had been forced to term *fear* for lack of any better word or preexisting knowledge.

God*dammit*. This feeling was supposed to be an illusion she'd already conquered. This was supposed to be a hoax perpetrated by one of her pathologically unreliable elders—father, uncle, whoever. But here it was, coursing through her body again so suddenly, as though someone had mixed together every conceivable unpleasant sensation known to man and injected the sadistic concoction directly into Gaia's chest. Three parts excessive caffeine, two parts fingernails scraping against a chalkboard, two parts sushi-induced food poisoning, and a healthy dose of a good hard kick to the gut that had knocked the wind out of her completely.

Two things that clearly did not go together: passion and direct questions. Not only was Ed's question deeply disconcerting, but it also seemed to yield him the very opposite of what he was looking for. He wanted clarity. He wanted Gaia to speak straight from her heart. He wanted her to tell him what she wanted. It was an excellent question. But what Ed got instead of an answer was her hopelessly childish, enigmatic silence.

Ready? How could she possibly answer such a question, given all the ludicrous and unbearable circumstances of her life just beyond Ed's closed window? Wanting it and being ready for it were two completely different things. How the hell could she know if she was ready for something she'd never even experienced?

In most categories, Gaia's knowledge exceeded that of the average department head at an Ivy League university. But in the category of actual sex. . . Well, her *knowledge* was sufficient—late night cable and the World Wide Web had made that nearly impossible to avoid. But her experience? That is to say, her *actual sexual* experience. . .

13

That would fall under the mathematical heading of Absolute Zero. As in, she had none.

This moment was where all her book knowledge left her behind. This was where reality diverged from fiction. Couldn't things just fade to black now? Like they did in the movies. Wouldn't that have been perfect? Right in the middle of their most passionate moment. Maybe right after she'd pulled his shirt off his chest and breathed the words, "I think so." Boom. Right there. Fade out. Cut right to the next morning.

But no. That was a tad unrealistic, wasn't it? In reality it seemed that sex wasn't just about love and passion and "the perfect moment." No, in keeping with Gaia's usual misfortune, she'd been introduced to fearlike feelings just in time to discover that sex was also apparently. . . rather scary.

"Gaia," Ed said softly, sliding his fingers down her cheeks and gripping her shoulders with the purest kindness. "You don't have to say anything, okay? We could just lie here like this for the next fifty, sixty years without talking, without doing *anything,* and I'd be happy."

Speak, Gaia, she implored herself. *Make sounds.*

"I don't even want you to say anything," Ed insisted. "I only asked you because it just felt like we were headed toward. . ." He stopped himself midsentence, seeming to reconsider what he wanted to say or at least how he wanted to say it. "I'm not in any kind of hurry," he said. "I mean, we're just sort of. . . starting here, and I wasn't even thinking about. . . Well, I mean, *yes*, I was *thinking* about it, but. . . we can wait for. . . I mean, we can wait as long as you want."

Tell him what you want, Gaia.

"Gaia. . . ?" Ed searched her eyes for signs of life. "I'm going to take your zombielike state to mean no. That you're not ready." He smiled at her, leaned his head forward, and touched his warm lips to the spot where her neck met her shoulder. "Though I would like to mention that you are immensely beautiful when you're pondering."

Ed reached over Gaia to take his shirt, which was balled up next to her. His smooth chest grazed over her, which only added to her state. Without even thinking, Gaia grabbed the shirt before Ed could get to it, leaving his body hovering over hers, even closer than he had been before.

"Wait," she insisted, feeling the heat of his face on her skin. "I just have. . . a few questions."

Ed looked slightly hesitant. He stopped reaching for his shirt and looked back into Gaia's eyes. "What kind of questions?" She was finding it difficult to focus with his body pressed against hers like this.

"Why?" she asked. "I thought I was the one who didn't like answering questions."

"No, it's not that," Ed said, "I just. . ."

"What?"

"I just don't think so well when we're this close.

15

What if I give the wrong answers?" The beautifully nervous look on Ed's face made Gaia feel far less settled. It also made him that much more irresistible. She had to force her hands not to latch onto his naked shoulder blades.

"They're easy questions," she said.

Ed paused for a moment to consider. "Okay, go."

"Okay. Question one: Are you aware that I am a *deeply* flawed human being?"

"Well aware," Ed said, smoothing her hair back from her forehead. His eyes moved across her face, seeming to savor each individual aspect separately.

"And do you understand that my life outside of this bed is. . . completely screwed up? I mean, *beyond* any kind of—"

"These are really easy questions," Ed interrupted. His smile nearly left her speechless, but she managed to gasp out the next question.

"And do you have a—a—" she stammered. "You know—do you have—protection?"

Ed looked almost offended by the question. "Of course I do," he said. "What kind of guy. . ." His face went blank in the middle of his own sentence. "Wait," he said, looking like he'd just gotten lost in the middle of some kind of maze. "Are you saying you want. . . ?"

"And do you trust me?" she interrupted him.

"Gaia." He shook his head with a disapproving smile. "*I'm* supposed to ask *you* that. Do *you* trust *me?*

That's how it works. You have to be sure that *you* trust *me*."

She didn't even see the point in that question. To describe how much she trusted Ed would have been redundant. To try and list all the reasons she trusted him would have taken too long. Of course she trusted him. More than she would be able or want to describe. Much like the way she'd realized she loved him and wanted him. Indescribable.

Gaia had known Ed longer than anyone other than her own parents. What she had with Ed had taken months to build. Months of slowly increasing trust and adoration. Months of conversations and confessions. Months of finding ridiculous and entertaining ways to pass the time together. Inept misunderstandings always followed by desperately needed reconciliation. The thought of separation always leading to a deeper connection. She didn't know a thing about relationships, but wasn't that exactly what all those things added up to? A real relationship. The realest kind. Not the thing that hit you like lightning and could slip away just as quickly, but something built much more slowly. . . with an unbreakable foundation. That's what Gaia had discovered here with Ed.

Maybe someone who didn't understand their relationship would have thought it was too soon, but something about this moment and this night. . . it just felt like the culmination of all their days together. Gaia felt like they'd broken through to the other side of something, and she didn't want to go back. She just wanted to keep going forward.

"Then yes," she said, looking into his eyes.

"Yes, you trust me?" he asked.

"No," she said. "I mean, *yes*, I trust you. . . but I meant yes to the other thing. The first question."

"What was the first question?" Ed asked.

"The one about being ready," she said.

Ed scrunched his brow, trying to keep up with Gaia's stream of consciousness. "The one about being ready. . ." She could have sworn she suddenly heard Ed let out an audible gulp as he gave her a look that bordered somewhere between awe and shock.

Ed looked deeper into Gaia's eyes. "Wait, I'm confused."

"Well, I'm not," she explained. "I'm not confused at all."

With that, she finally gave in to her own hands. She allowed them to caress Ed's chest, running her fingers around the contours of his back and pulling him to her with a deep, unbridled kiss.

Ed pulled his head back for a moment. But not to say any more. Only to smile at her. The use of words no longer seemed necessary.

He leaned back down, and he kissed her with a very different kind of kiss—a kiss that seemed to announce that something new had just begun. His hands became less careful and more confident as he pressed her body closer to his, rocketing her back into a state of full-blown shivers.

Those shivers. It wasn't until this moment that Gaia truly understood those glorious shivers. Ed had been under the impression that she was cold. Wrong. Gaia had been sure that her shivers were just the physical manifestation of all the joy and happiness coursing through her veins. That was true, but it was still only half the story. Once again she'd avoided the obvious:

She was shivering because she was *afraid*. And for the first time since her uncle's injection, Gaia finally remembered why she had yearned so much for fear in the first place. Yes, she had been happy before. Yes, she had even been ecstatic and overjoyed. But before fear had been introduced into her life, Gaia had never known what it felt like to be *thrilled*. Thrilled, the way normal, everyday people could be thrilled.

So much of her life had felt like a chess game up until this point. Even her fights. Always knowing her next move before she made it. Always knowing what *their* next move would be—always knowing what they planned to do to her next.

But this was nothing like chess. This was *so far* from chess. As Ed's hands slid so slowly down her shivering back and her hands floated along the center of his chest, Gaia finally understood that there was no way of being thrilled *without* being afraid. The thrill was born of the fear itself. It was the *not knowing*. Not knowing where her instincts would lead her or even which ones she might give in to. Everything she was about to feel was totally unknowable. That's what was making her shiver. And that was something she could only describe as... gloriously scary.

He grasped the top of her thigh as they rolled over together and forgot about anything beyond that bed.

And with each more passionate kiss, Gaia began to understand why those love scenes in romantic movies always faded to black—why the chapter almost always ended just before the act itself. It wasn't because the reality of sex was too scary or too "dirty." At least, not when it was right. It was simply that being with Ed like that... was too intimate to describe. Too close for any words or images to do it justice. It was something for only Gaia and Ed to know.

Ed froze like he'd just been zapped by an **deranged** alien space **wish** ray **fulfillment** in a C-grade Japanese sci-fi movie.

ONE CRISP, SUN-DRENCHED MORNING, two grande lattes, and Josh Brown. There could be no finer combination. At least, not as far as Heather was concerned.

Murderously Gorgeous

It was what Heather liked to refer to as a "Mary Poppins" morning. One of those mornings where the spirit of Walt Disney had not just taken over Times Square, but all of New York City, even below Fourteenth Street and down to the Astor Place Starbucks. The trees seemed to be politely stepping out of their way for her. All the rumpled, unshaven bohemians seemed to lock arms and dance a two-step down lower Broadway, while cartoon birds seemed to flitter down from the bright blue sky and perch on Heather's fingers, winking at her and exchanging whistled melodies as she floated into Starbucks.

Of course none of the above had taken place, but something far more dreamy and miraculous had: Josh's unheard of and all too daring Morning Follow-up.

Heather still couldn't believe it. She and Josh hadn't finished their previous coffee rendezvous until midnight last night. But at the end of that unbelievable evening, Josh had actually suggested that they meet again *the very next morning*. Nine hours. Nine hours between coffee dates. That kind of dating proximity was generally reserved for either deep, insatiable love affairs or desperately lonely people. And considering Josh's inhumanly beautiful appearance, she knew loneliness was simply not a possibility. *Not* that Heather thought he'd developed a deep insatiable love for her after one spilled coffee encounter and one semi-impromptu Starbucks chat. But nine hours? Even Romeo could wait more than nine hours to see Juliet. Things were looking awfully good.

And Josh was looking awfully good. His black T-shirt offered no distraction from his perfectly sculpted, angular face and arms and his slightly spiky, still wet from the shower jet black hair.

"You have got to be kidding me," he said, ducking his head in disbelief after Heather sat down at their sun-warmed window table.

"What?" she asked, widening her eyes with concern. Had she done something wrong before she'd even sat down?

Josh brought his head back up and stared at Heather, his eyes reflecting in the sun like blinding blue neon. "You can't look this good at nine in the morning," he said. "No one looks this good at nine in the morning."

"Oh." Heather smiled, feeling her feet melting into her Steve Madden shoes. "Well, I. . ." She could do nothing other than smile and look like an idiot. Was there any possible response to that? Probably there was, but not when Josh said it, there wasn't.

"You're one of *those,* aren't you?" he said.

"One of what?" she replied shyly.

Josh leaned forward on the table. "You're one of those girls who looks equally as beautiful when she gets out of bed in the morning as she does on a Friday night at seven-thirty."

"Okay, *stop,*" she giggled, averting her eyes from his murderously gorgeous grin. Silently, she prayed that he wouldn't stop.

"No, really," he went on. Her prayers had been yielding unprecedented success these last twelve hours. First he'd shown up at Starbucks last night after her wishful semi–stalker-like stakeout. Then came his suggestion of Morning Follow-up coffee. And now this. "Really. I bet you look like this the second you climb out of bed."

Now her legs had pretty much melted as well. When Josh said the word *bed,* Heather found it somewhat difficult to breathe, let alone put together a verbal response.

"I'm sorry," Josh said with an embarrassed chuckle as he leaned back in his chair. "Did that just come out as being ludicrously inappropriate? I didn't mean—"

"No, it's fine," she assured him with a nervous laugh. "It's just not true, believe me. I'm sure you look a hell of a lot better than I do in the morning."

Was that the right response? *Stay cool, Heather, you're losing your touch here.* Heather considered herself to have something of a Ph.D. in flirtation, but Josh was making it next to impossible for her to keep her feet planted on the ground. Perhaps that had something to do with the fact that he'd already melted her feet. And her legs, for that matter.

"Look, I'm sorry." He shook his head. Heather had no idea what he was sorry about, but she immediately felt her heart drop down into her stomach. Good Lord, this was bad.

"What?" she said, trying to mask her concern.

"I'm sorry, I just have to ask. . ."

"Ask *what?*" she whined inadvertently.

"Okay," he said, planting his elbows on the table with a confrontational glance. "When I found you here last night. . ."

Oh God. Busted. Totally busted. Heather grabbed her lukewarm latte and guzzled half of it down, looking for a calming jolt of caffeine. He knew she'd been waiting for him. He must have known that she'd been on a five-hour stakeout for him. She might as well have had a huge pair of binoculars hanging around her neck, a pith helmet, and a group of resentful natives carrying her supplies. She'd fallen down into the ranks of the hunter-explorer girls. The millions of non-self-respecting stalker skanks across the nation who lived for no other purpose than to entrap some unsuspecting *dude* and seduce their way into last-resort-late-night-hookup status with him.

"I just don't understand," Josh went on as Heather cringed internally. *Go on. Say it. Just say it.* "I don't understand what a beautiful girl like you could have possibly been doing alone at Starbucks last night."

Heather's head suddenly felt much lighter. Another compliment. Not the end of the line. Could she be any more sensitive? Any more of a full-blown loser? *Relax, girl. You're Heather Gannis, for God's sake. Never to be confused with the pathetic hunter skanks of the world.* She tried to shake off her panic as quickly as possible, hoping it hadn't shown through her long-rehearsed emergency smile.

"Come on, tell me the truth," he said with a sly grin. "Did you *just* break up with your boyfriend or something?"

She was so relieved to be undiscovered that she didn't even bother holding back with her answer. "Well, not exactly *just,*" she said, without even thinking. She guzzled some more latte to ease her sudden dry mouth. "It was a little while ago, but *after* we broke up. . . he kind of moved on to this other girl I know."

Ugh. That had been unpleasant to say out loud. Did Josh really need to know this?

"Ooh," Josh groaned with a comic wince. "Were you, like, good friends with this other girl?"

"*No.*" Heather laughed, looking more and more at her coffee. "Far from it."

She found herself wondering what Ed and Gaia were doing at this very moment. The last time she'd seen them, Gaia had actually gone pretty much berserk in the cafeteria, spewing out a totally uncharacteristic jealous tirade at Ed and her new Russian roommate (or something), Tatiana.

Watching them fight could have provided some kind of weird relief for Heather, as if maybe things weren't so damn heavenly in the world of Ed and Gaia. But the fact was, watching Gaia go nuts on Ed and Tatiana had only made Heather feel worse. Jealousy. It was the ultimate proof Heather had needed. If she'd had any doubts, now she knew for sure that Gaia was in love with Ed. Only love could make a girl go off on someone like that.

So what were they doing at this moment? They'd probably made up already. And two people are never more in love than when they make up after a fight. They make up. And then they have the makeup hug. And then the makeup kissing.

And then the makeup sex.

That's probably what they were doing at this moment. Having wild, passionate makeup sex. *Whatever. She doesn't deserve him. She doesn't deserve to know what it feels like to be with him. I was his first. There's nothing anyone can do to change—*

Whoa, Heather. New leaf! Where the hell is your new leaf?

Right. The new leaf that Heather had worked so

hard to turn over. She was through with resentment, and selfish thinking, and petty jealousy. New Heather didn't have those feelings. New Heather was Gaia's friend. New Heather tried to help Gaia out of a jam when she needed it. New Heather just wanted to see Ed happy—whoever he was with. Right? *Yes. . . yes, that's right.*

"Heather?"

"Huh?" Heather looked back up at Josh. His expression seemed to suggest that he was waiting on an answer to a question. Though Heather hadn't heard a thing.

"I said, are you jealous? You know, of this girl who stole your *man*," he joked.

Heather tried to answer before allowing herself to think further. "No," she blurted. "I'm not. . . . I mean. . . I'm really trying to stay away from that kind of thinking, you know. . . petty jealousies and stuff like that."

Josh's grin grew wider as he bored his stunning eyes deeper into Heather's. "Come *on*," he crooned, searching intently with an extremely cute little taunting glint in his eye. "It's not petty, Heather, it's *human*. You don't have to pretend with me, you know. You hardly know me. And I don't know them. It's the perfect situation to confess. *Confess*, Heather," he joked, pointing his finger directly in her face with the archetypal glare of the Grand Inquisitor. "Thou wilt confess thy jealousy."

Heather couldn't help but laugh. Gorgeous, smart,

and funny. She would have thought he was just a dream if his long, thick finger hadn't been pointing directly between her eyes.

"Well. . . ," she began with a half smile. "I did kind of used to. . . *despise* the girl."

"Ahhh," Josh exclaimed with a satisfied grin. He ran his finger down the center of Heather's nose, inducing a full-body tingle the size of Canada. "A little honesty. That's more like it." He leaned toward her. "Okay, Heather," he said with the mock seriousness of a Freudian psychotherapist. "This mystery girl. Let's discuss your hatred of this mystery girl. I think it would be very good for you."

WHAT TO SAY ABOUT THIS MORN-
ing. . . How to do it justice. . .

Body Tingle

Back in Ed's skating days, whenever he would take a massive fall, he used to leap right back up to his feet, grin from ear to ear, and scream out a hearty howl to the skies. As he would often explain it, he was announcing his total invincibility to the cruel and powerful gods of extreme sports. He didn't just want the gods to hear him, he wanted anyone in his general vicinity to listen. He wanted the world to be clear on his personal philosophy. Shred's Golden Rule: No setback was ever a setback. Life was something to be enjoyed and devoured at all times.

Particularly after his accident, people had always seemed awed by his ability to find joy in life no matter what the circumstances. They envied his ballsy nonchalance—his laughter in the face of near death, his humor in the face of self-pity and depression. He was a regular rolling bundle of joy. A French girl named Josephine had once told him he had *joie de vivre,* whatever the hell that meant. He was Shred—the eternal optimist.

But this morning, with his arm wrapped around the bare waist of a sleeping Gaia Moore, her tangled hair pressed against his cheek, her smooth shoulder peeking out from the rumpled purple sheets of his bed, Ed had begun to come to terms with something. Something he hadn't even quite known or recognized until now. Something he probably would have denied for years, if not for the rest of his life, had this morning never existed. And that something was this: His eternal optimism. . .

It had always sort of been work.

In fact, sometimes it had almost felt like his job. Maintaining that smile, lusting for life, howling joyously at the gods of misfortune. Staying happy. At times it had been exhausting. Because it really wasn't altogether true. That's not to say there wasn't a great deal of truth to it. Ed *did* have a kind of lust for life. He *did* find the joy and the humor in his existence at all times. But more of the time than he would have cared to admit, he was also kind of adding a little. Throwing in a joke when in truth he was in a crappy mood. Howling when he might have felt more like being silent or nursing his wounds.

In reality, he probably wasn't all that different from the people who supposedly envied him so much. He, just like them, had always experienced the slightest, almost imperceptible sensation of something missing in his life. There was always some kind of void he was trying to fill, something good old Shred might have been trying to cover over.

Until this morning.

The combination of the last perfect night and this glorious morning had clued Ed in to the fact that there was an entirely other kind of happiness. The kind he was experiencing at this moment. A happiness that did not require any kind of work whatsoever. One that did not require that he hide behind a joke or a daredevil stunt or a philosophy. There had simply been no way of understanding the void in his life until he knew the feeling of having that void completely filled. This morning marked the first time Ed had understood what it felt like to truly want nothing more.

He moved his head over Gaia's just to see her face— just to witness that golden, crisp detail that only morning sunlight seemed able to produce. If any part of their night together had been a dream or an illusion, the sun would surely expose it. The sun would set him straight.

But the sun confirmed that it was still Gaia resting against his body, sound asleep. Its glittering rays revealed every exquisite angle of her face. Every fleck of gold, bronze, and wheat hidden in her hair. The infant-like curves of her slightly too-small ears. The flush of light freckles that ran down from the bottom of her neck to the middle of her back. She wasn't a dream or a panic-induced hallucination. Not a fantasy or some kind of deranged wish fulfillment. It was the real Gaia. Unquestionably real. Their night together had been real. Everything they'd done together. . . real. He would be continuously replaying the night in his head for at least the next forty-eight hours.

In fact, watching the peaceful expression on her glowing face, Ed found her to look as real as he had ever seen her. So comfortably vulnerable. Goddesslike, yes. Always. But utterly and completely human.

And so, of course, the only way to honor such a goddess. . . was to make her pancakes.

"Gaia," he whispered, letting his lips graze her ear.

"Mm," she grunted sleepily, smiling out of the corner of her mouth. She turned her head slightly toward Ed's, keeping her eyes closed, letting her lips touch lightly against his. Maybe he didn't have to do pancakes just yet. . . .

"Are you hungry?" he asked.

"Mm," she croaked happily, living somewhere between sleep and waking. "Pancakes. . ."

Pancakes. Of course she wanted pancakes. She wanted pancakes and he wanted pancakes. He should have just proposed to her then and there. Instead he kissed her on the cheek and on the shoulder and pulled himself carefully from the bed.

"I'll be back in fifteen minutes," he whispered.

"Nooo," she groaned. "Don't go."

"I'm getting the pancakes," he said, pulling on a T-shirt and reaching for a pair of jeans.

"Hmmm. . . then you'd better go," she agreed. "But come back soon."

"Fifteen minutes," he said with a laugh. He grabbed one of his crutches and leaned down to her in the bed. "I'll be right back." One more kiss, and he started for the door.

"Okay," she mumbled sleepily, turning back toward the window and twisting herself into a ball under the sheets. "I love you."

Ed froze like he'd just been zapped by an alien space ray in a C-grade Japanese sci-fi movie. He turned around and took two giant strides back toward the bed. She'd sort of said it to him last night. And it wasn't that he didn't know it. They wouldn't have done what they did last night if she didn't love him. But she'd never really *said it* said it. Not like that. Not so sweetly and easily and simply. "What did you say?" he whispered.

Asleep. She was fast asleep again. But he'd heard it. He knew he'd heard it.

"Make it ten minutes," he said, even though she was asleep. "I'll be back in ten minutes."

SOMEONE ELSE'S LIFE. THAT WAS always how Gaia had experienced happy moments. She'd always felt like she was being granted a glimpse of some other life for a few hours, like she was in one of those ridiculous "switch" movies where two people exchanged bodies for as long as it took to learn a "valuable lesson." One of those ultracheesy eighties flicks where, due to some mysterious act of magic, she had temporarily awoken to find herself swathed in royal princess robes in some strange, faraway castle, while the *real* princess (who just happened to look *exactly* like Gaia) would be waking up in a tattered black sweatshirt and a pair of army pants in some dusty beer-stained corner of the Port Authority bus station. Which is exactly

Shiny Happy Couple

where Gaia would have been, were it not for Ed Fargo.

That was generally how happiness presented itself to Gaia. Like a very temporary magic spell. Like a beautiful illusion that could only be trusted for so long. As if the clock would strike twelve at any second and Gaia would wake up back in her own body again. Back in her dusty vintage clothes, trying to hitch a ride to Pittsburgh or something, while the true princess returned to her beautiful castle with her prince, having learned some valuable lesson, like how to flip a skinhead on his ass or how to open a can of tuna fish.

And that brief glimpse of someone else's life would be all Gaia had to sustain her for months as she traveled through her actual miserable life. A rather depressing take, she was well aware.

Only this morning was disconcertingly different. Gaia had finally given in to the blinding sunshine pouring through Ed's window and allowed herself to wake completely. But her first truly conscious moment was a strange and incredible thing. She was unmistakably blissful, but she was also unmistakably. . . herself.

She didn't feel as though she was inhabiting someone else's skin. She didn't feel as though the allotted time on her happiness clock had just started counting down. She got to fall in love with her best friend, spend the perfect night with him, wake up to a perfect morning c banter and pancakes. All those things were happening, but they weren't happening to "that girl"— that other person over there who was entitled to moments like these. They were happening to *her*, the actual Gaia Moore. And that was deeply, deeply bizarre.

She'd spent years training herself to lie still and let the pain wash over her. But for a moment like this one, she'd have to think back to when she was eleven or twelve years old. That was the last time she could remember lying still just to bathe in her own happiness. That was the last time she could remember a kind of happiness that didn't make her nervous, that didn't feel fleeting and precarious and moments from destruction.

There would be no disappearing glass slippers and no dress to return by midnight. Midnight had long since passed, and Gaia was still here. Breathing regularly. Joyful and still and grounded.

She stretched herself out in Ed's bed, extending each of her limbs to its limit, just as she would have at age twelve. She rolled her face into Ed's pillow, where there was still the slightest scent of his shampoo, and perhaps a touch of his soap, and something else. The faint but intoxicating sweet smell of his sweat. Or was it their sweat? The scent brought back a series of vivid physical memories from their early morning together, and Gaia suddenly found herself digging her head deep under the pillow with a certain gleeful embarrassment.

She knew there was nothing to be embarrassed about, but still, she couldn't imagine the shade of red her face must be under that pillow. Thank God, she was at least alone for this particular moment.

Sex. That was what was making her blush. Yet another thing she had come to believe was meant only for "that girl." That "normal young adult girl" over there with more than two pairs of shoes and a name that people could pronounce on sight. Somebody's prom date. The kind of girl who was entitled to major life-altering events that didn't revolve around superhuman genetics and national security.

But she was apparently very wrong about that as well. Because, as it turned out, she had something that no "normal young adult girl" had. Ed Fargo. And when the moment had finally come with Ed in the blue light of the very early morning, he had been just. . .

He'd known exactly what. . .

The blushing was out of control again. She could feel the heat emanating from her face, toasting Ed's pillow. Apparently she was too embarrassed to even finish certain sentences in her own head.

She could only go as far as to think of it this way: Whatever "fears" she might have had about her first sexual experience, Ed had put them all to rest. His sensitivity and his tenderness had made her feel so. . . safe. Was *safe* the right word? It was one of them. He'd made her feel much more than safe. All she wanted now was for him to get back to that room as soon as possible.

She finally removed the pillow from her face and reached down to the bottom of the bed, sifting through the tangled purple sheets until she located her T-shirt and her crumpled-up pants. She put them on under the sheet, and then she rolled out of bed, walking back around to the sun-drenched window to look for signs of his return. She shoved the window open as far as it would go and leaned her face out into the sun, letting in the chorus of New York morning sounds.

Birds were chirping from the sidewalk's trees, blending perfectly with the distant sound of a hip-hop beat pounding through loudspeakers from blocks away. Maybe a street fair? She leaned her head a bit farther out the window, where the smell of crepes, sausage sandwiches, grilled corn on the cob, and fried dough combined, wafting gloriously, almost visibly through the streets and over the stoops of the old New York brownstones. The perfect moments seemed to be coming in droves. Maybe she and Ed could take a walk through the fair after breakfast?

Wait. Had she really just suggested that to herself? This next-morning-bliss thing was getting weirder by the second. She'd just comfortably placed herself in yet another of those idyllic relationship scenarios from the world of the Shiny Happy People, where the only thing more utopian than the combination of sex followed by morning brunch was the combination of sex, followed by morning brunch, followed by a leisurely walk through a street fair while holding hands.

Gaia had witnessed this Shiny Happy Couple phenomenon several times at street fairs while she'd been waiting in line for chocolate crepes. The man was always wearing roomy shorts and a sweater regardless of the weather. The woman always in low-hanging pants and a formfitting shirt regardless of the weather. Both with designer sunglasses, both with slightly mussed-up postcoital hair. Both holding hands loosely and *always* walking slower than everybody else, as if they no longer *needed* to get anywhere now that they'd found each other.

When Gaia had first come to the city, this kind of brazen display of togetherness had made her ill. It had seemed so self-congratulatory. So in your face. But now here she was, picturing herself and Ed holding hands as they meandered through the street fair, perusing cheap imitation South American sundresses and tables covered with refrigerator magnets, totally unaware of any people other than each other. Did she have no shame? Pretty soon she'd be picturing them searching for loft apartments in TriBeCa and the perfect golden retriever.

Apparently being in love had the hypnotic effect of turning you into one of "them." One of those "other people" that Gaia had spent the last five years of her life simultaneously despising and envying. It was more than a little freaky. But Gaia didn't mind so much. Especially not this morning. As long as Ed would turn into one of "them" with her, she'd be happy. They could turn into artsy New York intellectuals, or faux punk runaways, or even yuppies in search of the perfect cappuccino. Gaia didn't really care. As long as Ed was with her, she'd be willing to try just about any future.

As if on cue, Ed appeared at the end of the block, lit up by the glaring sun as he smoothly carried himself home on his crutches with a shopping bag dangling from his wrist. Should she call down to him? Would that just be too *Romeo and Juliet/West Side Story*? No, she was through worrying about what role she was playing or where the real Gaia fit into this situation. She wasn't a sixteenth-century naïf and she wasn't a Latina by any stretch of the imagination, nor was her singing voice much to speak of. No, she, with her rumpled-up clothes and desperate need for pancakes and sausage sandwiches, was most definitely Gaia. And he, with his rumpled-up hair and bold, confident strides despite his crutches, was quite specifically none other than Ed.

"Fargo," she called down to him. But the combination of street sounds and distance left him unable to hear her.

He continued his fast-paced leaps down the block, totally unaware that he'd nearly jabbed the man walking behind him with his crutches. The man flashed Ed a dirty look, shoving his hands stiffly into the pockets of his black suede jacket. A classic frustrated response to the oblivious Ed Fargo. "Ed," she called down again. But he still couldn't hear her.

And when the man behind him pulled the gun from his coat pocket and aimed it directly at the back of Ed's head, Ed still couldn't hear her screams. There hadn't even been a split second to warn him.

ED WOULD NEVER KNOW WHICH THING

Private Frequency

he'd heard first: the sound of Gaia's desperate voice screeching his name or the deafening gunshot in his ear. But something made him turn around to see the barrel of the gun, just centimeters from his eye line, as it went off.

A din of high-pitched screams erupted from various corners of the street as the man repeatedly fired his gun. But all the screams seemed to echo from so far away. No one rushed toward him to help, shot after shot. No one came near the man in the black coat with the gun in his hand and the robotic sneer on his face.

Ed's crutches gave out under him as his legs buckled and twisted him off balance. He heard himself scream, "No!" as his right crutch scraped across the asphalt, sweeping the man's legs out from under him as they both collapsed to the ground.

There had been no time for thoughts. No time for his brain to tell his limbs to move. Just chaos. That was all Ed's brain could register. Loud, horrible sounds in his ear. Only the slightest comprehension of being *shot*—of being suddenly murdered in broad daylight, for no reason. His field of vision was flipped on its side as his head collided with the sharp sidewalk, only adding to his confusion. In front of him were the tangled arms of his assailant and the thick black handle of the gun. Behind him was a sudden stomping sound coming from a distance like a mild earthquake, vibrating throughout his entire head as his ear stayed painfully pressed against the rugged gray street.

That's the gun, he registered semiconsciously, staring at this oddly static image of the oversized smoking weapon that had shot him. He couldn't see his blood anywhere. He still couldn't feel where he'd been hit, but he'd know that soon enough. For now, only one thing mattered. *Still alive,* Ed assured himself, repeating the fact again and again in his head as he tried to breathe. *You're not dead yet. Not dead yet.*

But a moment more and he realized how many precious seconds he'd wasted already. It had taken that long for his brain to catch up with him. *The gun. Grab the gun, Ed, or you're dead for sure.*

He could hardly feel his legs, but he had to squeeze something out of his arms. The gun was within his reach if he could focus long enough to wrap his fingers around it. He reached out his half-numb arm, trying to latch onto the butt of the gun with his fingers. But the man in black was way ahead of him.

With no handicaps to impede him, the man swiped up the gun before Ed even had a chance. He jumped back to his feet in one smooth, seamless motion, and quite suddenly he was towering over Ed's splayed-out body, aiming the gun down at the center of Ed's forehead.

"Don't," Ed uttered uselessly.

The man couldn't have cared less. He looked at Ed as though he were nothing more than a faceless dummy with targets X'd off from head to toe. Ed could see the complete absence of compassion in the man's black eyes as he stared up at him helplessly in this frozen moment in time. He knew that the sight of this man's cold and hideous face would probably be his last. So in that last split second, he tried to picture Gaia's face. Gaia, who would now be left with absolutely no one. *Don't try to understand why this is happening,* he told himself. *You don't want that to be the last thought, either. Just picture her,* he shouted at himself. *Close your eyes and picture her.*

43

But that stomping... That stomping Ed had heard was getting closer and closer....

"Freeze!" someone howled from behind. "Put the goddamn gun down! *Now!*"

The man in black turned around for a moment. But only for a moment. He turned back to Ed, still expressionless, and thrust the gun even closer to his face.

That's when the first pocket of blood erupted from the man's shoulder. Four more booming gunshots echoed through the narrow street as black hole after black hole erupted in his chest, shaking his entire frame and pushing him farther and farther back on the street until his body collapsed just a few feet from Ed's, thin, vaporous smoke still rising from his wounds.

And every noise stopped. More silence than Ed had ever heard on a New York City block. The screaming pedestrians had shut their mouths. The gunfire was over. And no one had taken a single step. The man in black was dead. And Ed Fargo was still very much alive.

"Are you hit?" the gruff male voice asked from above. Ed stared up and saw the NYPD logo on the man's hat. A cop. That's who had saved his ass. Probably one of the same old street cops who'd been messing with Ed for years, back in his skating days. Ed couldn't for the life him remember how he could have ever had a problem with a cop.

"I... I don't know," Ed replied. "I thought..."

The cop grabbed Ed's shoulders and lifted him back to his feet, gathering his crutches and handing them back to him for support. He took a quick look all over Ed's body, frisking him from his back down to his wobbly legs. "You're not hit," he said. "I don't even see a scratch. Maybe a bump on the head."

Ed looked down and examined his body. He couldn't believe he hadn't been hit. He'd heard about people not even feeling the shots at first from shock or from all the adrenaline pumping through their veins. He'd assumed that's why he hadn't felt any pain. But apparently there wasn't a single wound. How was that possible? The first shot had seemed no farther than an inch from his face. And all those other shots. . . How could that coldhearted psycho have missed with every shot?

The sound of sirens replaced the silence as two police cars turned the corner, trailed by an ambulance from St. Vincent's. People on the street had just begun to inch closer for a better view of the dead body, but the cop stepped over and quickly began shooing them away.

"Step back!" he commanded. "Everyone just step back and let the paramedics through!"

Ed knew he still had to be in some kind of shock. Whether he'd been hit or not, he had still been quite sure he was going to die, and that left his mind spinning overtime. He found himself trying to run back through this totally random and horrific event. Where the hell had this dude come from? What the hell had he wanted? Just to shoot the first kid he saw on the street? Without a word? Without any anger or threats or anything? And then Ed remembered that the first thing he'd heard. . . had been Gaia.

Gaia. He'd heard her voice. Screaming at him. Trying to warn him. Where had that voice come from? Was she down here? Had she watched the whole thing? God, how had this perfect morning turned so unfathomably horrible? Where had her voice come from? Unless. . .

Ed turned around slowly, back toward his building, and looked up at his window. And there she was. Her stunning face and her morning hair leaning precariously far out the window, looking down at him. He grinned at her, trying to look less shaken than he actually was. "I'm okay," he shouted, stating the obvious.

Gaia seemed to smile slightly with relief, but there was something else in her expression. He couldn't even begin to understand the look on her face. Maybe it was too far to really see. Or more likely, she, too, was in some kind of shock after watching this whole thing go down. But from what he could read at this distance, she didn't exactly look relieved or happy or even worried. From this distance. . . she looked sad.

Ed felt drawn to her as his crutches seemed to involuntarily carry him back toward his building. Heading back home. He needed to get his arms around her as soon as possible and hold her for at least a few days.

In spite of his own near-death experience, he found himself suddenly feeling guilty. Gaia had put all her trust in him. She'd given herself over to him in spite of the fact that all the men in her life seemed to disappear, and here he'd almost disappeared himself. Not that it was even remotely his fault, but still, he felt an overwhelming need to reassure her. He needed to get to her as soon as he could. He needed to be holding her, and he knew she needed to be holding him. He was drawn another step toward his building.

"Hold on there, son," the cop shouted after him. "You're not going anywhere yet. You're going to let the paramedics check you out, and you're going to answer some questions, so you sit tight now."

Ed stood still, obeying the cop's orders. He tried to look into Gaia's eyes despite the distance. All the noise and the increasing crowd of shameless onlookers seemed to fade into the background as Ed and Gaia locked into their own private frequency. "Don't worry," he shouted, moving a few steps farther. "I'm *all right*. I'll be right up. I'll be up in five minutes. Maybe I'll climb up." He widened his grin.

Five more minutes and he'd be upstairs holding her, kissing her, touching her again. Five more minutes and, damn it, whether he'd almost been shot by a psycho or not, *they were going to have pancakes.*

A FEW GUNSHOTS. THAT WAS ALL GAIA had needed to remind her of who she was. Not who she'd hoped to be. Not who she thought she was finally becoming. But who she *was,* and what her life looked like. Her real life. A few shots and her whole ridiculous plan for the future came crumbling back down on her like an avalanche. The same ridiculous plan for the future she'd allowed herself to see with Sam. And Ed had nearly suffered the same fate.

The same mistake, Gaia. Again and again, the same mistake. Will you learn, goddammit? Learn, already.

It was really a very simple reminder they'd given her: *Stop hoping.* That was it. That was their message, whoever "they" were today.

Ed gazed at her from the street with his beautifully optimistic smile, and he told her that he was all right. He said it with his eyes, and he shouted it to her at the window. But Gaia knew the truth. He wasn't all right. Not as long as he was close to her, he wasn't. How could she have ever convinced herself otherwise? How could she possibly keep making the mistake of thinking she could get close to anyone? How could she continually ignore the lesson she'd been punished with time and again?

A few shots had woken her up from one of the best dreams she'd ever had. So it had been a dream after all. But that was all it could be. A dream. Just a perfect dream. And now it was time to wake up.

Memo

From: KS
To: L

    Operation unsuccessful. Target not terminated.
One casualty: KL now deceased.

Memo

From: L
To: KS

    On the contrary. Operation should prove one
hundred percent successful. Termination was not
the goal—only to free the subject of any further
distractions. This incident should successfully
sway the subject in the appropriate direction.
Orders are to take over KL's station and proceed
as planned.

How exactly
could being
ornery, cruel,
coldhearted,
and **monotone**
unshowered
make such **robot**
a favorable
impression on
intelligent
men?

"WELL, I ALMOST *DIED*," HEATHER said, gazing into Josh's gorgeous, attentive eyes. "Gaia wouldn't have given a crap if that psycho had cut off my head."

Pig Noise

"I can't *believe* that," Josh groaned, shaking his head. "She let you go bounding into the park, and she didn't say a word?"

"Not a word," Heather said. "Not even a *look*. And she knew who was in the park. She knew I'd probably end up slashed or raped or whatever. . . dead."

"And now you two are *friends*?" Josh squeaked.

"Well. . ."

"No way," Josh announced, slamming his coffee down on the table. "No way I could *ever* forgive someone for that. This girl sounds like Satan."

He turned away, looking totally indignant as he considered the extent of Gaia's injustice. Heather gawked at his perfectly cut profile as the sun poured through Starbucks' glass windows, casting all kinds of dramatic shadow patterns across his face.

Josh Brown was truly remarkable. Heather had been fully prepared for him to reveal himself as a bit of a macho asshole, a trade-off she would have been more than happy to make. It tended to come with the territory of someone so unmistakably manly. But Josh had displayed none of the usual drawbacks of a manly man. How could someone this good-looking be such a good listener? He was so much more sympathetic and attentive than Carrie or Megan. She couldn't remember the last time anyone had just sat across from her and listened so unselfishly for this long—not just listened, but actually *understood*. Remarkable. Truly remarkable.

"Well, what about your boyfriend?" Josh asked, turning back to her and leaning his elbows on the table. "I mean, if some psycho girl let my girlfriend go into the park, knowing she was going to be attacked, I would have gone looking for that girl, you know? I'd be looking for massive payback. Did your boyfriend tell her off, at least?"

Heather had tried not to give this question too much thought in the past months. Because the answer was so deeply offensive and embarrassing. But she'd been nothing but honest thus far in this conversation, and it had made her feel better than she had in months.

"Well. . . ," she began, "it was a different boyfriend then. Sam."

"*Sam*, huh?" Josh said, puffing out his chest to play the part of the jealous boyfriend. Heather giggled, thoroughly enjoying any reference, joking or not, to Josh being interested in her that way. It was something she still wasn't a hundred percent sure of, and any clues he gave her were deeply appreciated. Not to mention unhealthily exciting.

"Well, go on," Josh said. "What did *Sam* do? Did he give her a piece of his mind?"

Heather hesitated for a moment, letting her eyes drift down to her empty coffee cup. "No," she muttered. "Sam kind of ended up. . . going out with her."

"What?" Josh bellowed. An entire Starbucks full of East Village hipsters and NYU students turned in his direction. Heather pressed her finger to her lips with an embarrassed giggle.

"*Okay*," she said with a smile. "Calm down."

"What?" Josh howled again, still baffled and disgusted by Sam's behavior.

"Shhh." She begged him to lower his voice, but in truth, she had adored every ounce of his blustery volume. He didn't care how much attention he drew to himself. Sam's betrayal was worthy of a deep, disgusted shout, and Josh had recognized that instantly.

He obeyed her request and leaned in much closer with a private murmur. "This *Sam* guy sounds like a real wimp. I hope he's long gone."

"Oh, he is," Heather promised quickly. "God, I haven't seen him in ages."

"Well, maybe something horrible happened to *him* for a change. What goes around. . . and all that."

"Yeah," Heather semi-agreed, not wanting to wish Sam too horrible a fate. Though she had to admit, she wouldn't mind so much if maybe he fell on a little bit of bad luck.

"Wait, wait, wait," Josh said, leaning his muscular frame back in his little chair and crossing his arms.

"So let me get this straight. This Sam guy *and* this Ed guy *both* left you for this. . . this. . . what's her name? Guy something? Gynecologist?"

"*Gaia*." Heather laughed.

"*Gaia*. What is she, Finnish or something? Wasn't she in ABBA or Ace of Base?"

"They're Swedish," she replied between harder and harder laughs.

"Yeah, whatever," he said. "I bet her real name's Edith and she's just trying to be exotic."

Heather laughed and laughed until. . . *No way. It's too early.*

She'd been laughing so hard that she'd laughed her way into one of her most guarded secrets. *Her snort laugh.* She couldn't believe she'd just revealed her snort laugh to him. She could usually hold that back for months until she was absolutely sure that an `extremely rare pig noise` wouldn't cause a guy to reassess her completely. She'd never in her life trusted a man with her snort laugh so soon. But there was just something about Josh. Even though the duration of their relationship could still be described in terms of hours. . . she somehow already knew she could trust him completely.

And of course because he was Josh, her pig noise didn't send him running or even earn her a funny look.

"Okay, okay," he went on, "so you honestly expect me to believe that Sam and this Ed guy both left *you* for *her*?"

"Mm-hmm," Heather confirmed.

Josh threw up his arms. "Well, that just doesn't make sense," he said, as if it were the most obvious fact in the world. "She can't be prettier than you. She can't be smarter than you." Heather's entire body was now gurgling like an ecstatic baby. "She can't possibly snort as well."

"No," Heather agreed.

"So what is it? What the hell is wrong with these guys?"

Heather opened her eyes wide and considered his question. If she were to be totally honest with herself (which, thanks to Josh, she was being), then she'd have to admit that she thought it was a damn good question. Because in truth, in spite of all her attempts at turning over her "new leaf" and being less self-involved, Josh was helping to remind her of a very simple fact: Heather really couldn't fathom how a man could choose Gaia over her. How exactly could being ornery, cruel, coldhearted, and unshowered make such a favorable impression on intelligent men?

Heather had only one theory. A theory she'd been careful not to share with a soul since it did sound quite ludicrous. But in Josh's case, maybe she could make an exception. Josh just had this amazing power to make her feel. . . justified—*validated* in some way that she'd been sorely lacking ever since. . . well, ever since Gaia Moore had set foot in the Village School.

That's how long it had been since Heather had felt like herself. She decided to go for broke and share her secret theory. If anyone would stick with her on it, it would be Josh.

"Well, I think. . . ," she began carefully, "and I'm totally serious here. . . I think she hypnotizes them."

"Oh, really?" Josh laughed doubtfully.

"No, really," Heather insisted. "It's like she casts some kind of spell on them that convinces them that she's so *special*. I swear, it's like they think she's *super-human* or something."

"Well, is she?" Josh asked.

"*No,*" Heather replied, not totally sure if she believed her own answer. "I mean. . . *whatever,* the point is, they obviously didn't realize that *I* can be superhuman in my own ways."

"Oh, *really?*" Josh laughed suggestively.

"No, I didn't mean *that,*" she squawked. "Or. . . maybe I did," she admitted. She dropped her face in her hands to indicate embarrassment when, in fact, some part of her was feeling rather proud. She was back on her flirting game, and she knew it.

"Wait a minute," Josh said, straightening his posture as he eyed Heather with mock suspicion. "Is that why I had to see you again this morning? Are you casting some kind of spell on me like your friend Gallagher?"

"*Gaia.*" Heather laughed, locking eyes with Josh.

"And *yes*. I just made my Josh voodoo doll last night. I am now controlling your every move with my mind."

"Of course," Josh said. "And that's why I. . ." He cast a blank, zombielike stare over his eyes as if he'd been hypnotized. "I must meet you here again tomorrow night."

"*Exactly.*" She grinned, wondering if she might be able to find a private corner where she could literally jump for joy if not engage in a full series of cartwheels. She'd known her theory wouldn't scare him away. If anything, it seemed to have done just the opposite.

"And that's why I must. . ." He clamped his large hands to the small Starbucks table and began to shake his body as if some unearthly force had taken control of his will.

"What?" she begged.

"Can't stop myself. . . I must. . ."

"*What?*" she pleaded, widening her eyes with nervous anticipation.

He finally shot out from his chair, causing Heather to jump slightly in hers. He leaned across the table and kissed Heather on the cheek, letting his warm lips linger on her face before he pulled away. Heather's body heat must have increased at least twenty degrees. She tried to steady herself as best she could.

He stood up and rattled his head a few times. "I'm sorry," he said, as if he'd just awaken from his trance. "I—I had to do that."

"Of—of course you did," she said, straining

desperately not to leap out of her chair and throw her whole body onto his like a sex-crazed koala bear. "I told you," she said shakily. "I'm. . . I'm controlling your every move."

"Why does that not bother me?" Josh remarked. "Eight o'clock, tomorrow?" he asked.

"Yes," Heather replied, using every last ounce of her feminine wiles to appear nonchalant.

Josh flashed her his overpowering grin and then he made his way to the exit without another word.

Heather sat in her seat for a moment, trying to answer one very important question for herself. And finally the answer came to her. *The bathroom.* That wass a perfectly acceptable place to go jump for joy. She shot up from her seat, hoping she could make it there before she started doing back flips right in front of the milk-and-sugar table.

Memo

From: L
To: J

Provide status report on subject B.

Memo

From: J
To: L

Preparations for subject B are progressing
smoothly. Project may take even less time than
anticipated.

THE STAIRS. WHY THE HELL HAD ED

Amnesia

taken the stairs? Because the elevator in his building was taking too long, that's why. Every additional minute of waiting had felt like slow murder.

Jeez. *Brilliant choice of words.* He wondered how many more times the word *murder* would be popping into his head unnecessarily. Probably as often as the images from twenty minutes ago were flashing through his memory. The thick black gun in his face. The ugly, robotic glare of his unexplained executioner. The sight of a man being punctured with bullets as his erupting body was driven to the ground. *Get it out of your head, Fargo. Stomp it out.*

That could have been Ed's lifeless body on the street if that cop had shown up five seconds later. The thought of it was weakening his limbs, sapping what little energy he had left. But if he could just haul his ass up those freaking stairs and get back to her, then everything would be okay. He was sure of that. He just wished he hadn't been quite so traumatized as to think that the stairs would get him to her faster.

Brilliant move. Nothing speedier than climbing the stairs on crutches.

Right now he would have sold his soul to be rid of the crutches. Anything to be able to pump his legs up those steps like it was three years ago. Leaping them in twos and threes, hoisting himself over the railings if he had to. That's what he needed. He needed whatever it would take to get back into his room and back into his bed with Gaia.

Because that would be the cure: to simply delete the horrific incident and pick up right where they had left off twenty long and painful minutes ago. It would be just like pressing rewind. That was the only way he'd be able to stop his brain from spinning and his heart from reeling.

In fact, he was living it in his head already. It was helping him to drag his shopping bag and his clumsy butt more quickly. He could feel her hair against his cheek and the curves of her back spooned against him. The sunlight pouring through the window, lighting up her face.

Most important, he could hear the last words she'd said to him. The brilliant simplicity of those three words never ceased to amaze. Not to mention the way she'd said them. Totally unencumbered. Totally natural. As if she'd said them a hundred times before. That was where Ed planned to pick things up. Right from the moment that those three perfect words had fallen from Gaia's lips.

He finally stumbled onto his floor, panting like an exhausted racing hound. *Hallelujah. Home sweet home.*

The overly painted stairwell door slammed behind him as he bounced his way down the dingy brown carpet to his apartment. He ripped open the front door and made a beeline for his bedroom—just a few yards from replacing the quasi-soothing images in his head with her real flesh and her real eyes, and her warm arms wrapped around his neck.

"Honey, I'm home!" he shouted, dropping the shopping bag in the living room. "How was your day?" he called out, turning into the hallway. "Mine was the usual. You know, waking up with the girl of my dreams, getting shot at by a psycho lunatic. . ."

Ed cut his comedy routine short when he entered his room. He'd expected Gaia's arms to be wrapped around him before he'd even stepped over the threshold. He'd expected some tears of relief and an intense, suffocating bear hug that went on for five minutes without a word. He'd at least expected her to play along with his little domestic bliss number.

But what he got. . . was the back of her head.

Gaia was crouching down on the floor, searching under his bed. He waited awkwardly at the doorway for another beat as she pulled out her shoe and finally turned to him.

"Are you okay?" she asked. Her tone of voice was almost the exact same as the paramedics had used. Urgent and deeply concerned, but detached and efficient. Professional, even. Ed wasn't at all sure how to respond. He smiled at Gaia, thinking that perhaps she might be messing with him. But she didn't crack the slightest smile in response. Nor did she make the slightest move in his direction.

"Uh. . . yes," he said finally, almost shrugging. "I'm fine." He sensed she was looking for a direct answer. She didn't seem to be looking for the touchy-feely response. In fact, she seemed about as far from touchy-feely as a person with a beating heart could be.

"Good," she said. She stood up and paced the perimeter of his room, peeking into the corners and under the furniture. "I can't find my other shoe."

Ed stayed glued to the doorway, following her with his eyes, unsure what to say. Had she been so traumatized by the last twenty minutes that she'd been struck with amnesia and forgotten their morning together? Maybe his recent brush with death had already slipped her mind? "Are. . . you okay?" he asked cautiously.

"I'd be better if I could find my other shoe," she replied.

"It's under the desk," he said.

Gaia turned to his desk and grabbed her shoe. "Thanks," she said.

She brought both her shoes back to his bed and sat on the edge as she struggled to pull each one on. Ed stared at her in this most bizarre and unexpected silence, watching her tie her shoes.

"Are you. . . going somewhere?" he asked.

"Yeah, I really have to go," she said.

64

What? What the hell was she talking about? What was the game here? Ed didn't get it. Or maybe he just didn't know how to play?

"Go where?" he asked.

"Out."

The one-word response felt like a sharp elbow to the face. Silence was just about the only thing Ed could come up with in response. He began to rack his brain, trying to understand what on earth had happened to her since he'd last seen her in the window. "Gaia. . ."

"Yeah," she said, sifting through a pile of clothes in the corner of the room.

"Gaia, what are you doing?"

"I'm looking for my jacket," she said.

"No, I mean, what are you *doing*?" He stepped closer to her.

Her body swiped against his as she escaped eye contact and searched the other side of the room. "I just *told* you. I'm looking for my *jacket.*"

Ed gave in to another bout of silence as he studied every movement of her body, from her rushed, shaky gestures up to her cold, darting eyes. Okay, whatever this was, he could talk her back to earth, he was sure of it. Seeing him almost get shot must have induced some kind of post-traumatic shock or something, and he just needed to bring her back to that room. Because even though this cold and brittle girl might look like Gaia, it was obvious that the real Gaia had exited the building and left some monotone robot in her place.

"Maybe I should introduce myself," he said, stepping toward her with his hand extended for a shake. "I'm Ed. Ed Fargo. Your best friend. The guy you had sex with last night?"

"Ed, please," she mumbled, stepping away from him again.

"Ah, wait," Ed continued, "perhaps you know me as the guy who was almost murdered downstairs. Does that ring a bell?"

"That's not funny," she snapped, shooting him a vicious glance. "There's nothing funny about that." The look in her eyes cut painfully to the center of Ed's chest. She was right. It wasn't funny. But at least she'd shown an actual emotion for a second. Though one second later she was ice-cold again. A complete stranger wearing Gaia's skin.

She stopped in the middle of the room, slapped her hands on her hips, and let out a frustrated sigh as her eyes scanned the room. "Where is my goddamn jacket?" she asked with a groan.

"It's on the goddamn door," he said, stepping behind the door and ripping the jacket off the hook. He held it up for her at the doorway.

"Thank you," she shot back, stepping closer to him and nabbing the jacket from his hands.

"You're welcome," he muttered pointlessly, still

trying to cut through her dense mental smoke screen.

"I'll check in with you later, okay? To see how you're doing." She crammed her arms through the sleeves and made a move for the hall, but Ed planted himself in the center of his doorway, blatantly cutting off her escape route and leaving their faces much closer together.

"Can you stop this now, whatever this is?" Ed begged. "Can you tell me what the hell is going on?"

Gaia stared at him blankly. "I just *told* you, I have to go."

Ed waited, hoping there might be more. But there wasn't. He searched her eyes more deeply. "You've got to be kidding me."

"Well, I'm not."

"Okay, fine," he conceded, trying the `play-along-with-psycho-Gaia technique`. "Then tell me why you're leaving."

"Because I have to," she said, turning her eyes away.

"But *why?*"

"What are you, four years old?" She groaned. "I'll talk to you later, okay?"

"Jesus Christ!" Ed hollered. "I just got freaking shot at, Gaia. Do you think maybe you owe me a little more than this? Do you think after last night you might have a little more to offer than your old-school cold-and-pissy routine?"

Gaia's head dropped straight down toward the

floor, every hair on her beautiful head hanging over her face. "Don't yell at me, Ed," she insisted. Was she insisting or pleading? Ed couldn't even tell. Especially without seeing her face. Her voice sounded so tight, like she was forcing every sound out from her tonsils. "Just let me go, okay?" she asked quietly.

Ed tried to tip her chin up to look in her eyes, but she backed away from his touch and crossed her arms—the clearest piece of body language in the world. Translation: Don't touch me.

"Gaia," he sighed to the side of her face. "Twenty minutes ago, we were. . . What am I saying, you were *there*. Weren't you there? I was coming back here to make you pancakes. And on the way I had one of the worst experiences of my life since my accident. So that's *best* experience in my life, followed by *worst* experience. Either way. . . I don't see how you could *possibly* leave this room right now."

"I'm sorry," she uttered in that same strained voice. He could see her jaw clenching again and again under her skin.

"Don't be sorry, just tell me what *changed*. I don't get it."

"Nothing changed, I just have to go—"

"*No*," Ed moaned, slamming his hand against the frame of his door. "The truth, I mean. Tell me the real reason you're leaving."

"That is the real—"

"*Spoken honesty,*" he interrupted, grabbing her shoulders and trying to get a lock on her eyes. "We were working on spoken honesty, remember? Tell me the truth, Gaia. The truth. It can't be *that* hard."

"Okay, fine!" she snapped, batting his hands off her shoulders. "The truth is. . . I just feel. . ." Her eyes were darting from corner to corner of his room—the ceiling, the floor, her hands, anywhere but his eyes. "I just feel. . . weird about. . . what happened, and I think. . . maybe it wasn't the right thing to do." She barely had enough breath to finish her sentence.

Ed leaned in to try and see her eyes again. "You're lying," he said.

"No," she croaked. "No, I'm not." Her head fell perpendicular with the floor again. "I'm just. . . not sure I feel. . . *that way* about you, and. . . and I think that what we did. . . was a mistake."

"This is bullshit," Ed said with a resentful giggle. "You're talking crap, and I know it. Where'd you get this speech? *Dawson's Creek* or something?"

There was no way. There was just no way she was telling the truth. He'd seen her face that morning. He'd heard her words. It had been the perfect moment. Two completely content people who'd finally found each other for real. Two people who wanted pancakes. There was no way he was going to let her rip their perfect night to pieces just so it would match the rest of her life. No way. If what she was saying was true, then why were tears beginning to fall from her supposedly uncaring eyes?

"It's not bullshit," she growled as a tear streamed down her cheek. "It was the wrong thing to do, Ed. That's it. That's all of it. We did it and it was a mistake, and now I want to *leave*."

"I just don't—"

"I don't give a shit if you believe me or not!" she shouted. "And if I'd known you'd be such an arrogant asshole about it, I would have just snuck out while you were gone. Now, can you please just let me go?"

She shoved Ed out of her way, shot right past him, and ran for the door. She had the front door slammed shut within three seconds. And that was that.

But. . . *what was what?* What the hell had just happened? Everything coming out of her mouth had sounded so false, but her anger was so unquestionably real.

What if she *was* telling the truth? Was that possible? Ed felt a sudden painful gnawing in his stomach as he stared at his quite suddenly empty room. If that was the case, if she'd actually meant all the god-awful things she'd just said to him. . .

Then Ed had just suffered two attempted murders in the last twenty minutes. And Gaia had been far more successful than the hideous man in the black suede coat.

Official Letter of Resignation
and Surrender

To whom it may concern
(including such parties as my
uncle, my father, the Fates, God,
and Satan),

I'm sure it will please all
the aforementioned parties to
know that I, Gaia Moore, do
hereby officially resign and
surrender to your bullshit. I
know I've made the same mistake
time and time again, but I want
it made abundantly clear that I
will no longer make that mistake. You win. You will no
longer need to torture me or my
loved ones in order to remind me
that I am not entitled to a
relationship or a remotely happy
or normal existence. Because
your message has been received.
Loud and clear.

In case the above statement is
not clear enough in and of
itself, here is a more detailed
list of activities and emotions I
promise never to engage in again.

GAIA

    I, Gaia Moore, swear to never
again:
-Fall in love;
-Wish for a boyfriend or a family;
-Become too close to anyone (as
 that would result in their death
 or disappearance, as it did for
 my mother, father, Ella, Mary,
 and Sam);
-Continue any kind of relationship with Ed Fargo; or
-Be hopeful or optimistic in any
 way.

    In exchange for these guaran-
tees, I ask one thing and one
thing only. That you do not harm
Ed Fargo in any way, shape, or
form. That he is permitted to
pursue a normal life of his own
completely free of the Curse of
Gaia Moore, as I will refer to it
from now on. I'll never know for
sure if that ugly bastard with
the gun was actually sent to kill
Ed or just to send me a warning,
but it really doesn't matter.
I'll never know for sure which
one of you sent him (uncle,

father, Fates, God, Satan?),
though I'm pretty sure that I can
narrow it down to two possibilities (as in the two despicable
humans in that list), and that
really doesn't matter, either.
All that matters is that Ed has
suffered enough undue torture in
his life, including the very
poorly executed pack of lies I
was just forced to yell in his
face, thus obliterating one of
the greatest mornings of my life.
I have now left him alone (as per
your barely cloaked demands), so
you have to do the same. You have
to leave him alone. You have
taken Sam, and that is enough.

I would also like to put down
here for the record—not that it
will matter to you, but just so
the truth exists somewhere other
than inside my head—that I am
completely in love with Ed Fargo
and know in my heart that what we
did last night was not a mistake,
even though you've so kindly
reminded me that my getting too
close to anyone is a mistake. I

do not think I will ever love
anyone in quite the same way that
I love Ed, especially given the
fact that you have already taken
Sam Moon away from me. And I am
more than happy to resign myself
to a permanent state of misery if
it will guarantee that Ed has a
chance at a normal, happy life.
(I'm quite sure he will get over
me in no time, as who in their
right mind would not?) In fact,
the moment I left Ed's room, I
immediately began the "permanent
state of misery" plan, and you'll
be glad to know I've only stopped
crying long enough to write up
this agreement. Then, I promise
you, I'll go right back to crying. That or beat the shit out of
some asshole on the street (I
hope you'll still allow me that
one minimal pleasure in life).

   I would also like to state for
the record that if you do not
hold up your side of the bargain,
if Ed is harmed in some way even
after I've broken my own heart in
a trillion pieces by avoiding

him, then I will find you and I will kill you. That also is guaranteed (assuming you're one of the two people I think you are).

So let's hope we have a deal here so that I can move on with my miserable, pathetic life, Ed has a chance at happiness, and you can all go to hell (with the exception, of course, of you, Satan, for obvious reasons).

Now, if I just had somewhere to actually mail this freaking thing. I'm not sure how to get an exact address for God or the devil. I don't think "heaven" or "hell" would do the trick. Then again, finding an address for my father or my uncle would be just as hard.

Gaia Moore

In her new,
officially
lonely life,
there was only **mr.**
one **streaks**
remaining
solace, and **and**
that was the
kicking of **tips**
degenerate
ass.

GUILT HAD QUICKLY BECOME A SIDE

Shameful effect in all of Tom's meetings with Natasha. Almost instantly. There was no question that they had a certain undeniable chemistry. A chemistry that two world-class agents *should* have had no problems overcoming.

But at each meeting, Tom had found the task of overcoming his guilt just a little more difficult. And for some reason, tonight the guilt had officially become more than a side effect. Maybe it was just sheer exhaustion or the disheartening lack of progress in his investigation, but after one drink at this seedy bar with no name on Clinton Street, Tom's guilt had left the realm of side effects and become a full-blown disease.

He wasn't sure what was troubling him more, the fact that he was in New York City and keeping it from his daughter, or the extent to which he'd begun to look forward to these covert midnight meetings with Natasha. No, of course he was sure. Keeping his whereabouts from Gaia was for her own benefit. Exactly who was benefiting from these late night briefings was becoming less and less clear. As long as Natasha was living with Gaia and taking care of her, she would be Tom's only connection to his daughter. So of course he wanted as many reports as possible about what took place on the home front. But these meetings had begun to feel like more than just agent to agent, and Tom knew it.

"Tom. . . ? Are you all right?" Natasha inquired. Even her elegant Russian accent was becoming a distraction.

"I'm fine," he replied, offering only as much eye contact as was absolutely necessary. "Sorry, I'm just checking through my notes."

"Of course," she said. "Take your time."

"So she came back this morning?" Tom asked. As long as they only discussed Gaia, he could keep the guilt in check.

"Yes. She left Ed's house, and she was home by about eight-thirty or nine this morning. And she stayed in her room the entire day, Tom. It was so unlike her to stay in our house for so long. She didn't leave her room until about eight o'clock this evening. I imagine she's headed out for her usual 'roaming.'"

"I'm sure," Tom agreed, shaking his head. He wished that somewhere along the way, Gaia had developed a hobby other than self-appointed vigilantism. But he supposed it was his own fault. He'd spent so many years preparing her for the worst that the worst was really all she knew now, all she was comfortable with. Yet another parenting mistake to add to Tom's endless and fast-accruing list.

"But I tell you, Tom," Natasha added, squeezing his hand on the table, "she looked even more sullen and detached than usual, as if something had upset her so terribly. Just the look on her face was enough to break my heart. I can't blame her at all for not wanting to speak with me."

Here was another disgusting example of Tom's growing problem with Natasha. Once she had placed her delicate hand over his, he'd missed the entire second half of her statement. And he was no longer making an effort to avoid physical contact, either, as he'd attempted to do in their earlier meetings. Because her touch was comforting, and he was too tired tonight to deny it. He could only deny so many things at the same time.

Once she removed her hand from his, it was much easier to focus again.

"Do you think she and Ed had a fight?" he asked.

"I am sure this is so," Natasha agreed. "A very bad one. Very bad."

Tom felt a sudden wave of nausea pass over him. "Oh God." He sighed quietly.

"What is wrong?"

"She's doing it, too," he murmured, half to himself.

"She is doing what?"

Yet another shot of guilt right in his heart. *The sins of the father...*, Tom thought. Gaia was cutting herself off from the outside world, one person at a time. He was sure of it. He could sense it just from the few details Natasha had given him. Soon she'd have absolutely no one left, and she'd learned that very self-destructive skill from her father. A horrific method of coping he'd apparently taught her by example: Detach yourself from people, and people don't get hurt. One more mistake to add to his list.

"I just can't stand the thought of them fighting," he said, staring down at the table. "She's already lost Mary Moss and Sam Moon. I think Ed's the last friend she's got. And God knows she doesn't have her *father*. I know that's what she thinks."

Tom tossed his notebook down on the splintered wood table and began to rub his tired eyes with his palms. He generally did everything in his power to keep all forms of negativity at bay, as it was enormously counterproductive. But the last few days had chiseled away at his defenses to the point where he'd allowed himself to appear this unprofessional in front of Natasha. It was shameful.

He knew his brother had given Gaia some kind of potentially harmful drug, and there had been nothing he could do about it. He knew Gaia was falling further and further into a solitary world, and he had no control over it. Not only were his failures as a father showing more clearly each day, but Tom was seriously beginning to wonder just what would be left of the warm, ebullient daughter he'd known when all of this was over. *If* it was ever over.

Meanwhile, Tom had been so deeply ensconced in

rubbing his eyes with uncharacteristic self-pity that he hadn't noticed that Natasha had pulled her chair much closer to his to comfort him. He didn't even realize she was there until he felt her hand on his right shoulder.

"I thought the *Russians* were worriers," she joked, massaging his shoulder. "You must trust that things will work out. Gaia will be okay. We will *all* be okay. You must trust me, Tom."

Once again Tom was struck with the immediate, impulse to pull his shoulder from Natasha's kind touch. And once again tonight, he didn't move a muscle. Tonight he was simply too weak to resist or pretend that it didn't soothe him.

"I just can't have her living a solitary life," he said, bombarded with images of Gaia all grown up, living in the thousands of hotel rooms and classified locations where Tom had spent the majority of his life after Katia had died. "I can't have it."

Natasha cupped his chin in her hand and turned his face to hers, examining his eyes. "*Hmmm,*" she huffed.

"What?" Tom asked, doing his best not to be mesmerized once again by her kind eyes.

"This life you fear for Gaia," she said. "I think maybe it is *your* life you are speaking of, uh? This solitary life. . ."

She was also quite perceptive. "Is it that obvious?" he asked.

"But Tom, is it not also obvious that. . ." Natasha

stopped herself and pulled her hand from his face. "I'm. . . I'm sorry," she breathed as she began to pull her chair back.

But something took hold of Tom's will. Maybe it was his weakened state or just a bout of temporary insanity—or temporary sanity, he wasn't sure which. Or perhaps it was just a sudden burst of plain old-fashioned yearning. Whatever it was, something made Tom reach out his arm and grab her chair before she could pull away.

"Wait," he said. "What were you going to say?"

"No, it's all right," she gasped. "I didn't mean to—"

"Please," he interrupted. "I want to know what you were going to say. Really."

For one fraction of a moment Natasha looked as openly shy as a five-year-old child. Her eyes widened, and her confident professional demeanor simply fell away.

This beautiful, professional woman, with one of the most dangerous and deceptive jobs on earth, had somehow managed to preserve some aspect of her innocence. And when it revealed itself, it was a beautiful sight. Beautiful in every sense of the word. In those moments she was just. . . remarkable. Truly remarkable.

"All right," she agreed, leaning back toward him as she slid her silky hair behind her ears. "I was going to say that once again, I think you worry too much.

About your daughter and about yourself. This solitary life of yours. . ."

"Yes?"

"This is a choice, Tom. This does not have to be your life. Take tonight, for instance. . ." She leaned closer to him. "Is it not obvious to you yet. . . that you don't have to be so alone?"

Tom stared at her bold, unmoving eyes. She was proving superior to him in every aspect. Both more innocent *and* more brave. He was so amazed by her bravery, he didn't even know what to say.

"Oh, dear," Natasha moaned, placing her hands on her cheeks. "Now I think perhaps *I* have been a little too obvious. I'm sorry, Tom. That was inappropriate of—"

"No," he interrupted her. "No, *don't* be sorry. Don't."

In matters of national security, Tom had more courage than most, but in matters of the heart, he'd only recently begun to understand what a coward he could be. And for just a long enough moment, he finally stopped his mind from spinning with guilt and he let her bravery inspire him.

"You're right," he said. "You're right. I don't want to be alone." He reached out his hand and ran his knuckles gently down the curves of her face. "No one deserves to be this alone."

She fixed her eyes on his as he ran his hand through her hair, which was every bit as much like silk as it had looked. And finally he kissed her. For better or worse, he tasted her lips, and it was as human as he'd felt in a very long time.

BARE-BONES EMOTIONAL SURVIVAL

was now the name of the game. And that meant very little thinking, no feeling, and absolutely no crying under any circumstances. That meant that no thoughts about Ed or their crapped-on Shiny Happy New York Couple

Someone to Stomp

future were permitted into Gaia's brain. No thoughts about his lips, or his touch, or the perfect night she was straining so painfully to forget.

In her new, officially lonely life, there was only one remaining solace, and that was the kicking of degenerate ass.

Of course Washington Square Park was now completely out of the question. All aspects of her previous life would now be dropped into a large tin can, doused with gasoline, and set ablaze. Besides, she'd had enough of Washington Square Park. From now on it was out with the old and miserable and in with the new and even more miserable. Namely, the Upper East Side. Gaia's official and unbearable new home.

"Boring" could not begin to describe the Upper East Side. "Dead" would be a more apt description. With its massive gray-and-white tombstones of buildings and its empty streets at night, the entire neighborhood was like some rich old people's ghost town. Right now West Fourth Street was probably crawling with people. Drag queens and skate freaks. NYU film heads and Long Island imports looking to get drunk at the Slaughtered Lamb. People laughing, screaming, yelling. Drunk off their asses, but undoubtedly alive. Meanwhile, Gaia had consigned herself to the stark, windy silence of East Seventy-second Street, with nothing to hear but the echoes of Ed's voice in her head and her usual self-hating mantras: *You're a freak of nature. You're a liar and a phony and a real bitch on wheels. You didn't deserve Sam or Ed, which is why this will be your life from here on out.*

In fact, there was only one saving grace of her new life on East Seventy-second Street. And that was the vast uncharted territory of Central Park, which was where she'd ended up tonight, drifting through dark paved walkways and wide-open fields.

She had officially decided that Central Park would be taking Washington Square Park's place as her new stomping grounds. And she was desperately looking for someone to stomp.

Central Park was the ultimate bipolar park for the ultimate manic-depressive city. In the light of day, it was a sunny, windswept paradise of sorts, filled with hearty bicycle riders and disco rollerbladers. Children laughed and frolicked on the old carousel. Rock bands jammed in the wide-open amphitheaters. Shakespeare was performed outdoors next to a grand old castle. And lovers took rowboats out on the scenic pond while hippies baked under the sun in the grassy expanse of Sheep Meadow.

That was in the light of day.

By night, Central Park was something entirely different. It turned into a den of degenerates, gangs, and general assholes. A place where drug deals were always being made and women were most likely being targeted by perverts in the bushes. A place that was too dark, poorly policed, and generally avoided by anyone in her right mind at night. It was exactly what Gaia had been looking for.

Only tonight she'd had no luck. No screams in the night, no gang rapes to break up, no knife-wielding skinheads of any kind. Not even your basic run-of-the-mill eighteen-year-old mugger. It was hard to gauge distance in this massive expanse of landscaping and twenty-foot rock formations, but Gaia figured she'd probably traveled at least ten blocks in the near darkness, and she'd seen nothing but trees, two passed-out homeless guys on a bench, and the occasional jogger. She'd heard nothing but wind, rustling bushes, and the din of crosstown traffic. Apparently her life had become so empty, she didn't even deserve the pleasure of kicking a man where it hurt.

This, it seemed, would be her new life. Long, pointless walks in the park and then back to her beige-and-cream girlie bedroom with Natasha and Tatiana—her fretful fake mother and her supremely annoying fake sister. Her new family of complete strangers. Maybe it was time to just skip ahead to the old folks home now and live out her life in curlers and a lawn chair, staring at daisies and waiting for her next liquid meal. Because Central Park was all she had left. And apparently `everything she'd heard about it being a crime-ridden hellhole at night was a bunch of crap.` Either that or the mayor had just done such a bang-up job with additional cops that there was no one left for her to save. Central Park, it seemed, was just a park.

At least that's what she was thinking until she heard an enraged, muffled scream in the distance.

She instantly swung her body around to follow the sound. With each step she took, the woman's screams became louder until. . .

"Get your goddamn hands off me!" Suddenly they were only a few feet away. She was much closer than Gaia had thought at first. "Don't you freakin' touch me!" the woman howled.

Gaia had only one thought:

I love New York!

She took off toward the sound of the screams, heading toward the light pouring through the trees ahead.

"Will your shut your mouth?" a man shouted back as Gaia jumped a tangle of shrubs and leaped through a slim space between two trees. She landed in a crouched position and tried to get a better view of the scenario.

It wasn't just one guy. There were three of them. Three "dudes" with ridiculously macho hairstyles and thigh-length leather jackets. Two of them had the girl pushed up against a big rock while the tallest one had his hand on her neck and his body sprawled all over her. They looked like young pimp wanna-bes. Or some not-ready-for-Hell's Angels looking for something to do. Gaia couldn't get a good look at the girl yet, what with her assailant mauling her so thoroughly. But that was about to change.

Gaia was oh so ready to pounce. She was totally juiced up on adrenaline—the cure for all that ailed her. She checked herself for good mental preparation, and then she leaped out from the bushes, walking toward the triumvirate of Guidos.

"Are you okay?" she asked the girl, trying to sound as innocent as possible as they all turned their heads in unison.

The tallest dude peeled himself off the girl and whipped his head around, holding a thick hunting knife in his right hand.

Okay, one knife. Good to know.

"Keep walking," he warned with a strong outer-borough accent. Everything about him read Brooklyn Tough Guy, with the exception of the platinum blond streaks and tips atop his dark brown, lubed-up hair. He couldn't be much more than twenty. His friends looked older and much bigger.

Gaia's eyes turned to the girl, who was in dirty black jeans and a black hooded sweatshirt—had she raided Gaia's closet? She was pretty, in a goth sort of way, probably no older than nineteen. Even her hair had been dyed black, with the very notable exception of a huge streak of extremely fake-looking red flowing down in the front. Gaia couldn't quite read the girl's expression. She was probably too scared to ask Gaia for help. She probably didn't see how Gaia *could* help. But that was about to change, too.

"I just wanted to make sure she was okay," Gaia said.

"Oh, I'm *sorry*," he replied sarcastically. He turned back to the girl. "Are you *okay?*" he asked, in a fake-mommy singsong.

The girl didn't reply. She only looked back into Gaia's eyes nervously.

"I guess she's fine," the dude said, looking back at Gaia and turning his knife in his hand. "I'm not so sure how *you're* gonna be if you don't turn your ass around and get out of here."

"No, I'm fine," Gaia said firmly, locking eyes with this asshole.

"No, I don't think you're *hearing* me," he hissed. "Get your nosy bitch ass out of here!"

"I'll just wait till you're done," she replied calmly.

He threw back his head, nearly laughing with frustration. "Bitches!" he groaned. "What is it with the bitches tonight?"

He began marching toward Gaia furiously. His buddies followed close behind, giving her easy access to them. But when they pulled out their knives, all three picked up speed.

That's when there was a sudden unexpected hitch in Gaia's chest. And a horrible dry lump in her throat. And a stinging queasy creak in her stomach.

No. No, goddammit. There's no way this is happening again.

What a horrible way to be reminded of Ed. Just when she'd found a truly viable distraction, here was the same miserable sensation that had frozen her like a Popsicle in Ed's bed. The "fear" thing. The "paranoia-like" thing, or whatever the hell it was, started gnawing at her chest again, pounding in her head, making her feel ill and weak. All Gaia knew was that it always picked the absolute worst times to present itself, like when she was about to be attacked.

Who on earth designed this whole fear thing? And are they trying to get us all killed?

A few more steps and they'd be right on her.

This was supposed to be the moment when Gaia zinged into focus. This was when her heart rate used to slow down in preparation. Now it was pounding its way out of her chest. *Focus,* she scolded herself. *Overcome it. You said this was what you always wanted, remember? To overcome fear. So you damn well better do it right now.*

The first man lunged for her stomach and, thank the Lord, even though she'd heard herself let out an embarrassing gasp, her reflexes still kicked in. She dodged the knife, clasping her hand around the platinum asshole's wrist and flipping him over her shoulder. He was a lightweight compared to the other two.

Her heart was still pounding way too quickly, annoying beads of sweat leaking all over her palms. She could actually feel her legs begging her to run. Her legs wanted no part of this battle. But she willed them to stay planted to the ground.

The bigger Guido swung next, and Gaia was barely prepared. She just managed to sidestep to her right and crouch low to the ground. Even her eyes were locking up on her. It was harder to see the angles, harder to pick her moments. She wished she'd met up with these losers before fear had been introduced into her life. They were amateurs. She should have had them flat on the ground twenty seconds ago. But everything was taking longer with all her heart palpitations and hesitation. She was moving too slowly to win.

Finally the angle came clear to her and the best combination presented itself. Gaia worked quickly and desperately before she could manage to screw herself with all this sweaty hesitation. Staying low to the ground, she launched a sweeping kick to the legs of the biggest thug, sending him toppling straight into the knife of his leather-clad twin. He let out a throaty scream that terrified both his partners and sent them running at full speed.

Thank God, she groaned to herself. She knew she hadn't had much left. If that move hadn't worked, this pathetically fearful fight might very well have been her last.

After a few more seconds of writhing around, the remaining thug finally lumbered his way off the ground, trying to grab at the minor wound on his back as he turned and followed his buddies.

Of course, Mr. Streaks and Tips shouted out a bunch of vengeful yammering as he ran, employing the word *bitch* at least twenty more times. But Gaia was so relieved to be alive, she barely even noticed. And fearful or not, she'd still managed to plant the seed in his mind that his "bitch ass" wasn't so invincible. That was something.

More important, the girl in black was alive and still fully clothed. Whatever he'd hoped to do to her tonight, he'd failed. Gaia walked back to the girl, trying to catch her breath as her heart rate finally began to return to normal and the knots in her stomach began to untangle.

Even the aftereffects of this fear thing were a pain in the ass. Obviously she needed to understand it a hell of a lot better than she thought she had. Was her uncle's injection for real or not? Given that she had no idea how to reach her uncle *or* her father, that was something of a moot question, wasn't it? She didn't want to think about it, anyway. What was the point of trying to figure something out when there was no way you could get the answer? *Don't think*. That was still the new policy.

"Are you okay?" she asked, crouching next to the girl, who was still sitting on the rock.

"Yeah," the girl said, sighing with frustration. "Thanks. Thanks a lot. That was some serious *Karate Kid Five* shit. Where'd you learn that?"

"I just watch a lot of Bruce Lee movies," Gaia muttered.

"Yeah, well, you gotta teach me that flip thing sometime. That shit would *really* come in handy." She pulled out a pack of Marlboros and popped one in her mouth, offering the pack to Gaia. "I'm Genevieve," she said. "But no one calls me Genevieve." The girl was awfully relaxed for someone who'd just almost gotten raped. In fact, she seemed more pissed off than upset.

"Gaia," she replied, trying to catch her breath. "I

don't smoke," she added. "What *do* they call you?"

"Gen," the girl replied. "*Gaia?* What the hell kind of a name is—"

"Don't ask," Gaia muttered.

Gen shrugged and shoved the pack back in her pocket. She leaned her face closer to Gaia's. "Hey. . . are *you* okay?"

"Yeah, I'm fine," Gaia said, breathing heavily, trying not to feel quite so woozy. Throwing fear into the mix had made the fight a hell of a lot more exhausting, even if it had only lasted a minute. But something about this Gen girl had already made Gaia not want to appear weak in front of her. She just seemed to have more balls than the average female. Who did that remind her of? She reminded Gaia of someone. Someone besides herself, that is.

"You're *sure* you're all right?" Gen asked again. "You look a little messed up."

"Oh, yeah," she replied, lying through her teeth as her vision began to dim. "I'm fine. But, uh. . . if it's cool with you. . . I'm just going to pass out for a minute."

"Cool." Gen nodded, taking another puff on her cigarette.

Who did Gen remind her of? Well, no time to figure it out now. Gaia nodded her thanks and then watched as Gen's face turned an ugly shade of brown. And then there was just blackness.

"PLEASE TRY TO REFRAIN FROM YOUR

Imperfection

inane questions to-
night," Loki warned
as he sat down in his
chair with his lap-
top. "We have a great deal to cover, and I've only got a
few minutes for this briefing."

Josh handed Loki his coffee and then walked across
the wide bare floor to the leather couch. "Understood,"
he said with a whimsical smile as he plopped down on
the couch.

His childlike demeanor made Loki pause with
annoyance before sipping his coffee. He waited impa-
tiently for Josh to appear more attentive, but the
Cheshire-cat grin wouldn't leave his face. It was as if
Josh had told himself a joke that he simply couldn't get
over. Not only was it unprofessional, but it was also
rather offensive, given the seriousness of all the various
matters at hand.

"Would you like to wipe that childish grin off your
face?" Loki finally requested.

Josh widened his eyes as if he'd been unaware that
he was smiling and quickly shifted his expression to
something more appropriate. "I'm sorry," he murmured with compensatory seriousness.

Loki made sure to glare at him for another few
seconds just to be sure Josh would rid himself of any
further distractions. "Can we proceed?" he asked,

disgusted by the need to act as Josh's kindergarten teacher.

"Yes, of course," Josh assured him. "I'm sorry. I wasn't aware I was smiling."

"Fine," Loki said, sipping his coffee and turning one of the few lamps in his sparsely furnished loft closer to his laptop to examine his notes. "Now. . . the matter of the Fargo boy seems to have been handled."

"Yes," Josh agreed. "I understand she hasn't made contact once since early this morning."

"Yes, well, after your debacle with Sam Moon, I thought it better to nip this in the bud."

Josh lowered his head in shame and gulped his coffee. "I'm sure you're right," he mumbled, still much too childishly as far as Loki was concerned.

"Besides," Loki added, "there's no reason Gaia should have to suffer through another painful situation like the mess with Moon. This separation is going to be far better for all parties involved. Excessive attachments would only complicate matters."

"I agree," Josh said.

Loki froze again before sipping his coffee, flashing Josh another disapproving glance. "I didn't ask for your opinion," he said flatly. He kept his eyes locked with Josh's until he was confident that his point had been received. Josh let out a brief, uncomfortable sigh and scratched the back of his head.

"I'm sorry," he said, not so convincingly.

Loki eyed Josh for another moment, trying to

assess what might have gotten into him this evening. His lack of decorum was disheartening, to say the least. And his smiles could be described as nothing other than "goofy." Loki had spent just about all of Josh's life training him and his "brothers," and while he understood that one must always leave room for error, Josh had been chalking up more than his usual share lately. Particularly with the Moon fiasco. There was no question that Josh's usual perfection had taken a serious dip as of late, and it had left Loki with a needling sense of concern. It was more than just the errors; Josh had also displayed a few unfortunate bursts of attitude. Nothing particularly out of the ordinary, but still, given the scope of the new operation and Josh's significant role therein, his mild foray into imperfection would need to be remedied immediately.

"Josh," Loki said, leaning forward in his chair, "do you think we're developing a problem here?"

Josh sat up straighter in his seat and dropped the lighthearted air from his expression. "Absolutely not," he stated.

"You're sure?"

"*Yes*," Josh stressed with emphatic assurance. "As a matter of fact, I think things are moving along quite smoothly."

Loki shared one last silent moment of intense eye contact just to be sure. "All right," he said kindly, removing the excess tension from their conversation. "Tell me how smoothly they're going. What's our progress with the Gannis girl?"

"Well," Josh said, rising to refill his cup, "I think this one is going to be a piece of cake."

"Is that right?"

"Abso*lute*ly." Josh smiled. He took the long walk to the kitchen area. "I, uh. . . I really think I should take my time with this one, though." He kept his eyes glued to his coffee cup. "You know. . . just to be sure there are no mistakes. I think we may have rushed the Moon situation. I think that may have been the problem."

Loki rolled his eyes slightly. "Yes, I'm sure you'd *love* to take your time with this one, but we'll be doing just the opposite." He turned back to his notes. "I want to move far more quickly. That's the entire point of changing the plan."

"I don't understand," Josh said as he sat back down on the couch.

"Yes, you rarely do lately," he muttered, looking over the latest batch of reports from the geneticists. "You do recall me asking you to refrain from inane questions?"

Josh slammed his coffee cup down on the floor and stood up. "Well, with all due respect," he complained, "I don't know how you can expect the best out of me when you keep me in the dark half the time. Maybe if you provided *a little* more information to begin with, you might see my margin of error decrease. Not to mention those little 'bursts of attitude' you've mentioned."

Loki removed his reading glasses and looked up at Josh's indignant and somewhat demanding expression. He felt ready to pounce on yet another display of insubordination. But in truth. . . Josh had a point. "Perhaps you're right," he conceded.

Josh's expression relaxed, as did his breathing, from the look of things. "Thank you," he said, sitting back down in his seat. "So. . . why the rush?"

"Because the doctors are ready," Loki replied, unable to mask a very slight proud smile.

"They are?"

"They are." Loki sat back in his seat more comfortably. "The preliminary tests on Gaia's DNA samples are done. And the doctors have already engineered the serum."

"Already?" Josh replied with wide-eyed amazement.

"Already," he confirmed with a smile. "So you ask me why we're rushing? My answer is *because we can*. You understand now? This is precisely why the shift in plans. We no longer *need* to invest years of laborious effort and training into a complicated cloning experiment that could only develop at a snail's pace. If we've captured what we need in this serum, then we'll have the proverbial 'lightning in a bottle.' The financial possibilities would be limitless. Not to mention the political possibilities."

"So. . . you're abandoning the second-generation experiment altogether?" Josh's eyes suddenly looked rather hollow.

"Isn't that what I just said?"

"Yes. . . but I thought—"

"Yes, I know what you thought; that's why I'm filling you in, as per *your* request, yes?"

"*Yes*, but. . ."

Loki was beginning to get impatient. He'd wasted too much time trying to educate Josh. It really wasn't necessary. Josh's task at hand would be the same regardless.

"The missing piece is really in your hands," Loki stated, giving Josh his most serious and demanding glance. "As I said, the serum is ready. The doctors are ready to test a genetic transfer on a new subject. So, you tell me. . . how long before the Gannis girl agrees?"

Josh still seemed preoccupied or troubled by something.

"*Josh*," Loki snapped. Josh quickly shot back to attention. "Do I need to ask you again? Are you and I having a problem?"

Once again Josh adjusted his demeanor accordingly, ridding himself of distractions and childish expressions. "No," he said. "No problem. No problem at all."

"Then how long?"

"Well, all your intelligence on Heather was right," he replied, relaxing in the couch and beginning to act much more himself again. "She's obviously insanely jealous of Gaia. I think she'd absolutely jump at the chance to be like her in any way she could. It'll take a little bit of finessing, but I'm willing to bet she'll take the bait in two weeks, maximum. Probably less."

Loki was extremely pleased with the estimate, and he let Josh know so with a smile. "Fine," he said, leaning back comfortably. "That's fine. Then we'll move ahead now with the plans for the Caymans."

"Okay."

Loki looked back to his laptop, making sure they'd covered all the necessary bases. "Good," he said, trying to suppress the wave of excitement running through him. "That's very good. Everything seems to be very much in order."

"Definitely," Josh said.

"Regarding Tom and Gaia, our new field agent is now firmly in place. We should now have full inside access to both of them. When the time is right, our agent removes Tom. . . and we have no further impediments to this operation."

Memo

From: G
To: L

Subject is still unconscious in the clearing behind the Met. Should some action be taken? Please advise.

Memo

From: L
To: G

Be patient. As long as the subject is under your supervision, everything will be fine. Obtain as much information as possible and provide a full report.

FIRST THERE WAS JUST THE DIRT

Four

under her nails. That was all she could feel. And then against her face, scraping her cheek and her ears, crusty dirt crawling into the corner of her mouth. The smells were green like earth and spoiled like garbage. But as her eyes began to flutter open. . .

No, that's certainly not possible. That's not right. More hallucinations? Oh God, please tell me I'm through with the hallucinations. Maybe a dream?

The more her eyes began to focus, the less she was able to deny it.

Ancient Egyptian ruins were towering over her. They were glowing in golden shades of sand and stone. Somehow she was floating between two worlds. All around her it was night, and she was surrounded by grass and filthy earth. But in front of her. . . sand and Egyptian temples lit up by the sun.

Welcome to La La Land, Gaia. You've finally lost it.

No, wait. Glass. A huge wall of glass between her and the Egyptian ruins. What did that mean? A wall of glass. . . was that some kind of symbol? She knew she should have studied those goddamn Freudian dream books.

Her focus improved a little further. It was about thirty more seconds before she branded herself an idiot.

The museum, you idiot. You're staring at the back of the museum.

Of course. The Temple of Dendur at the back of the

Metropolitan Museum of Art. She must have seen it at least five times from the inside the museum. She'd just never seen it from outside the huge glass wall of windows. She put the pieces together as she rolled herself over in the filthy grass. That had been the light coming through the trees when she'd first heard Genevieve screaming. They obviously left the lights on in this part of the museum overnight. The scariest thing was that she hadn't even noticed this huge Egyptian temple the whole time she'd been dealing with Genevieve's Guido would-be rapists. *Get a clue, Gaia. Maybe you need to look around you once in a while.*

She took her own advice and opened her eyes a bit wider, checking in her immediate vicinity. The first thing she saw was Genevieve, still sitting on her rock, drinking a bottle of something. How long had Gaia been out? She couldn't believe Genevieve had waited with her the entire time.

"Hey," Gaia croaked from the ground. "I'm back."

Gen had one of those pager/text messenger things open, and she seemed to be totally engrossed in the message she was reading. She slammed her pager closed and shoved it in her pocket. "Hey," she said, taking a swig from the bottle and making a face of utter disgust. "Ugh. Man," she complained, spitting into the dirt. "Couldn't they drink a freakin' beer just once?"

"Who?" Gaia asked as she picked herself up and dusted the dirt off her already filthy clothes.

"The richies," she said, reaching into her pocket and pulling out her pack of cigarettes. "All the Upper East Side private school kids like to have their little 'hide from Mommy and Daddy' parties behind the Met. They think it's *way cool*. But they never drink any good freakin' beer. All they ever drink are *wine coolers*. I mean, *man*. Come on, people. Leave me something I can drink. Have you ever *had* one of these things?" She extended the bottle to Gaia. Gaia was still pretty queasy, and the sight of the bottle alone almost made her vomit.

"No, thanks," she said, wrapping her arm around her stomach and pushing the bottle away.

"I know, right?" Gen muttered, hurling the bottle into the bushes. She lit another cigarette and started to sift through the few other pieces of junk the "richies" seemed to have left behind. A crumpled-up bag of chips, a few more wine coolers, and the box to a Dave Matthews CD. "Now there's a good time," she said. "Wine coolers and Dave Matthews. Can rich kids party or *what?*"

Gaia huffed out a little laugh as she found another rock to sit on. Something about Gen's joke sparked a little memory in the back of Gaia's mind. It had an oddly endearing ring to it. . . .

Mary. That's who Gen reminded her of. It was the exact kind of joke Mary would have made. With just the same ironic inflection.

Gaia watched as Gen made sure she'd found everything the kids had left behind. When she was through searching, she picked up the crumpled Dorito bag and peeked inside, pulling out the few chips that were left and munching on them. She extended the bag to Gaia, who once again declined, fighting off another wave of nausea.

Gaia wasn't sure if Gen would be offended by the question that kept running through her head, but she had to ask it. "Do you. . . live here?" she asked cautiously. "I mean. . . in the park. . . ?"

Gen took her time before answering the question. Which was just about all the answer Gaia needed. Now she felt even worse about asking. Gen popped open another wine cooler to wash down the chips. "I live lots of places," she said, pretty successfully avoiding the question. "Ugh, *disgusting.*" She threw yet another wine cooler into the bushes.

Gaia was admittedly a little thrown. If Gen did live in the park, then she didn't fit the description of a homeless person that Gaia was accustomed to. She was far too pretty and far too young to not have *someplace* to go.

"So. . . ," Gen began, looking Gaia in the eye for pretty much the first time, "are we asking questions now?"

"Whatever," Gaia replied with a shrug.

Gen let out a loud and massive belch.

"Was that your question?"

"No." Gen laughed. Ugh, that was spooky. She even had Mary's laugh. "My question," she went on, "as long as we're asking questions. . . How long have you been using?"

"Using what?" Gaia asked.

106

"Yeah, right." Gen laughed. "That's my line, too. 'Using what, Officer?'"

Gaia was still drawing a blank.

"*Drugs*." Gen laughed again. "How long have you been using drugs? And don't even bother trying to tell me you're not a junkie."

Gaia didn't even know how to respond to such a ridiculous accusation.

"Oh, *come on*," Gen jabbed. "You're gonna try to tell me that's not why you came up here tonight? To buy from Casper?"

"*Casper?* Who the hell is *Casper?*"

"Casper," Gen said, as if it were obvious. "Casper, the dude you flipped on his ass, Casper?"

"You *know* him?" Gaia squawked.

"Yeah, I know him," she replied with a look of disdain. "I know that asshole. He thinks he's such hot shit with his leather jacket and his Sugar Ray *NSync ass. That was just beautiful when you kung fu'd him and his meatheads. Beautiful. You know, he's not so tough when you take away that knife and his thugs. Then he's just another punk dealer, you know? But he so deserved what you gave him. He so deserved it."

Gaia had never in her life thought of herself as unintelligent, but as she put all the pieces together, she couldn't believe how blind she'd been to the abundantly obvious. She hadn't saved Gen from getting raped in Central Park. She'd just saved her

107

from her pissed-off dealer. Ugh. Her *dealer*. Now she was *too much* like Mary.

Gaia took a much closer look at Gen and realized how completely strung out she was. How could she have missed it? This girl was, without question, a full-blown junkie. She was thin as a rail, pale and gaunt, with dark circles under her eyes, chain smoking, and digging around Central Park for leftover junk food. So how could a homeless junkie living in Central Park afford to pay for that pager? Who knew? Maybe *Casper* paid for it. Keep those customers coming back. That was probably why he'd gone off on her. Probably just pissed about some money she owed him or something. *Jesus.* Casper was just Mary's dealer Skizz come back to life. All dealers were Skizz. Greedy, pathetic assholes with nothing better to do than prey on helpless addicts.

The Mary connection suddenly made Gaia far more ill than it had at first. She couldn't help thinking. . . what if Mary hadn't had money? What if she'd had the same drug problem minus the incredible supportive family and the beautiful apartment on Central Park West? She'd probably be living the exact same life as Gen. And she probably would have died even sooner.

"So, come on," Gen said. "How long have you been hooked?"

"No, no," Gaia began, shaking her head.

"It's okay." Gen laughed. "I'm not a narc. Don't even try to lie."

"No, listen—"

"You're coming up here behind the Met all alone in the middle of the night. You were here to buy. . . ."

"No—"

"You're nodding out on me for twenty minutes. You're all pale and nauseous and shit. You're a freakin' junkie."

"*No!*" Gaia hollered finally. "No, I'm *not* a junkie and I *don't* do drugs! I'm not that stupid!"

The smile immediately dropped from Gen's face. She began to shoot hollow-tipped bullets at Gaia with her eyes.

Oh, no. All Gaia had wanted to do was set the record straight for herself. But she'd done a little more than that. Maybe, just for a second there, she'd kind of started yelling at Mary by accident. Now she'd ended up deeply offending this girl she didn't even know.

Gen took a long, slow drag from her cigarette. "*Relax,*" she spat coldly. "I'm really *sorry.* I didn't mean to call *you* a junkie. A pretty girl like you? Little Kung Fu Barbie? A pretty girl like you could *never* be a junkie."

"No, that's not what I meant." But it was obviously too late.

"Are you rich, Gaia?" Gen suddenly asked, looking her over with a piercing stare.

"No, I'm not rich." Gaia sighed, wishing there were some way to take back her stupid outburst.

"No? 'Cause I'm thinking you might be rich. I'm

thinking you might be one of those wine cooler kids who really ought to be getting her ass home to Mommy and Daddy right now."

Gaia dropped her head and scoffed at that suggestion. Gen didn't even know just how ludicrous it was.

"No," Gaia said with a smile that was so bitter, she could almost taste it, "there's no Mommy, and there's no Daddy. Mommy died. And Daddy disappeared. In fact, if you're really interested, there's *nobody*. No boyfriend. No friend. No polite acquaintance. Not even a dealer who beats me up. Just me, myself, and yours truly. . . and I guess *you* at the present moment. . . . Do I qualify for pity now?"

Gen went silent. Her eyes softened as a modicum of sincerity returned to her voice. "You don't know where your dad is?"

"No clue," Gaia said.

"Well, when's the last time you saw him?" she asked. Not the question Gaia would have expected.

"I don't remember."

"You don't remember the last time you saw your father?"

Gaia then remembered that she'd sort of seen him yesterday. . . or the day before or was it the day before that? But she'd been in such a feverish, hallucinogenic state that it had barely even counted. Gaia assumed Gen meant seeing him while conscious. "No," she replied. "I don't remember."

"Well, is he in New York City?" Gen pressed.

"*I don't know.*" Gaia groaned, baffled by Gen's sudden weirdness. "Why are you asking me all these questions about my father?"

"Whoa, there, buddy." Gen threw her hands out defensively. "I was just trying to be friendly. God knows where my pops is at. Maybe they're hanging together in deadbeat daddy day care."

"Sorry," Gaia mumbled. "Yeah, maybe they are."

Gen gave Gaia a once-over again with her eyes and then took another long drag, blowing it off to the side so as not to blow smoke in Gaia's face. "Hmmm," she uttered. "An orphan but not an addict." She stood up from her rock, flipped the red streak of hair off her pale, angular face, and stomped out her cigarette on the ground. "Well. . . I guess one out of two ain't bad. Are you hungry?"

Gaia looked up at her suspiciously. "Not for chips and wine coolers, I'm not."

"No, we can probably do a little better than that."

"Then yes, I'm starving."

"Do you have any money?" Gen asked.

Gaia sighed and shook her head. "Actually, no."

"Good," Gen said. "It's more fun that way. Tonight we eat like queens!" she pronounced as if a chorus of trumpets would follow. "Come." She beckoned with a grand sweep of her hand. Follow me, Kung Fu Barbie. Let's be *friends.*"

Well, I've mulled it over
for the past twenty-four hours.
In fact, that's all I've done for
the past twenty-four hours. That
is to say, I haven't eaten. I
haven't slept. I haven't exer-
cised, spoken, taken a walk or a
shower. I haven't done a thing
but pace my room and try to
understand what went wrong. Try
pacing on crutches in a rela-
tively small bedroom, and you'll
begin to understand the extent of
my twenty-four-hour purgatory.
    You know, I'd honestly seen
our whole future while I was
looking for butter at the A&P.
It's true. I had it all planned
out. Right after breakfast, I was
going to take Gaia to the street
fair on Avenue A. I'd pictured us
doing that New York couple *slow
walk* down the street. We'd look
at imitation designer sunglasses,
and horrible club-music mix
tapes, and giant collections of
copper farm animals. I don't
know. . . . I'd just pictured us

as a couple. A real couple with
this big, long future.

So I grabbed the butter, a gallon
of milk, some maple syrup, a fresh
box of Bisquick, and, of course, the
quintessential breakfast-in-bed
rose. And then. . .

I don't know. . . . I don't
understand it. Somewhere between
my getting shot at and walking
through my door, Gaia just
decided to rip out my heart and
eat it for breakfast instead of
the pancakes.

The question is, do I believe
everything she said to me or not?
Do I believe that she really thinks
what we did was a mistake? Do I
believe that she really doesn't
feel "that way" about me? I mean,
honestly, could my life be such a
miserable confounding joke that
five or six hours into our relationship, Gaia would *end* the relationship? After all the things
she'd said to me? After all the
time I'd waited for this to happen?

See, if I *did* believe everything she'd said to me, then I

wouldn't be in purgatory right now, I'd be in hell. Plain old hell. And then I could officially begin my new life as the most depressed son of a bitch in the entire Village School. I'd no longer be known as "Shred," but rather something more along the lines of "Bed," because I'd hardly ever leave mine. Or maybe they'd just call me "Dead," because, for all intents and purposes, that's what I'd be. Maybe I'd even get back into the chair just because walking required too much energy. At least that's a pathetic existence I could understand. Something I could learn to live with.

But like I said, I've been mulling it over, and the problem is, *I still don't believe her.* I still think there's some kind of hidden agenda here that she's keeping from me. Something about seeing me almost get shot or something I know absolutely nothing about that's making her lie.

To tell the truth, I think I'm

pissed. I mean as pissed as I can
be at someone I'm madly in love
with. I'm pissed at her for not
trusting me with whatever is
really on her mind. For kicking
my feelings around like a soccer
ball just because she's too
afraid to tell me something. For
leaving me here in purgatory.

So after twenty-four hours of
doing nothing but pacing, I've
made a decision: It's confronta-
tion time. I need the truth. If I
have to squeeze it out of her,
then so be it, but I need to
know. Because she owes it to me.
Just based on our friendship
alone, she owes it to me. And
even if it turns out that all
those horrible things she said
were true, I'd still like to know
that for sure. Because if I'm
going to be living in hell. . .
I'd at least like to plan ahead.

She might as
well have had
the phrase "I
have a **urban**
crush on Ed"
not–
embroidered
so–
on all her
perfect **chic**
little Calvin
Klein
outfits.

ED COULDN'T REMEMBER SITTING IN

Unadulterated Agony

a room so somber and silent since his accident. That's what Gaia's apartment felt like. A hospital waiting room. A place where all the family gathered and prayed that their loved ones had lived through the night. Of course all they were waiting for this morning was a simple phone call from Gaia Moore. But when Gaia was involved, the possibility of sudden death never seemed that far-fetched.

He couldn't even believe this was his second morning vigil with Gaia's phony family in just the last few days. The last time, Natasha had been a tad more relaxed about it. At least she'd pretended to be. She'd even served Ed cookies while they waited. But this morning she wasn't even bothering to fake a smile. This morning she looked downright anxious.

Tatiana didn't exactly seem all that concerned. She was sitting quietly at the dining table with her books in her lap, looking over one of her papers for school. But Ed and Natasha were sitting on the living-room couch, quite literally waiting by the phone, which Natasha had brought over to the coffee table so that it might be grabbed within the first ring.

117

"I don't understand it," Natasha said, staring at the phone. "I don't understand why she must do this."

Ed shook his head slowly, keeping his eyes pinned to the phone as well. "I think I've understood about ten to twelve percent of anything she's ever done."

"Yes, this is exactly right," Natasha agreed. "Why do you think she is like this, Ed? Why do you think she runs from people this way? Does she not understand that there are people in her life who love her more than anything in the world? More than they care for themselves? Who make all the choices in their life only so that she might be happy?"

Amen. Ed couldn't have possibly said it better himself. Natasha probably wasn't even referring to him, but boy, did that nail it on the head. Gaia seemed so utterly lonely so much of the time. But whenever she was alone with Ed, all her darkest thoughts seemed to drift away. Didn't they? Was he just making that up in his head? It had to be at least partially true. So, given that she always seemed less lonely when she was with him, *why did she always end up running away?* It was totally counterintuitive. And these little morning gatherings had made it quite clear that her surrogate family was suffering the same fate.

Ed was baffled as to why Gaia would run from

Natasha and Tatiana, who were, as far as he could tell, two of the nicest people he'd ever met. Again, it just made no sense. What could she possibly see in them that was so threatening?

Of course, the whole time Ed had watched Gaia deal with Natasha. . . There was that to consider. Ed had thought that Gaia's being `in a state of paranoid dementia` might have had something to do with her desperate need to stay away from Natasha. But now that Gaia had regained her sanity. . .

Well. Maybe that was the real question. Was Gaia back to normal or not? Because judging from the way she was dealing with Ed. . . at least as far as Ed was concerned, the sanity question was still way up in the air.

Natasha turned to Ed and breathed out a long sigh. "Ed. . ."

"Yeah?"

"Ed, if she were to ever return again—"

"Hold up, now," Ed said, forging a half smile. "I don't think she's gone for good." *Do I?*

"Well, no," Natasha said. "I don't want to believe this, either. This is why I want to ask you. . . *When* she returns. . . maybe, you might tell her. . ."

"Tell her what?" Ed asked.

"Tell her that Tatiana and I are *good,*" she said, widening her large brown eyes. "We are good, loving people, Ed. Tell her that she needs to *trust* me so that I might take care of her. And Tatiana also. So that Tatiana might look after her as well."

Ed's eyes darted over to Tatiana just in time to see her rolling her eyes with an inaudible huff.

"Well. . . sure," Ed said with a kind but useless shrug. "I'll tell her." What Natasha didn't seem to understand was that Gaia would need to trust *him* before he could convince her to trust someone else. And her trust in Ed was yet another issue that seemed to be flying somewhere way up in the air.

"Thank you, Ed," Natasha said, turning her attention back to the phone. "You are a good person."

"Yeah, well. . ." Ed thought they were going back into stare-at-the-phone mode, but Natasha suddenly turned to him again.

"Ed. . . as long as we are becoming friends waiting by the phone here, perhaps I might ask you a question that is too honest?"

Ed didn't exactly understand what she meant, but he couldn't see the harm in it. "Sure."

"Okay." She smiled, shifting her whole body in his direction and meeting his eyes. "I have heard that you and Gaia are good friends. That is what you have been called. 'Good friends.'"

"By whom?"

"I think you avoid the upcoming question." She smiled again.

"Oh. . . ," Ed replied, not sure if that's what he was doing.

"So, yes," Natasha went on, "you are 'good friends,' yet the other morning I saw Gaia when she came from your house. I was sure you two had been quarreling because she was so upset. More upset than any girl would be after quarreling with a 'good friend.' And the last time I saw you here. . . that very, very horrible afternoon. . . I distinctly remember Gaia referring to you as her '*boy*friend.' This is very different. So, perhaps you will tell me, honestly now. . . which is it? Is she your friend? Or your girlfriend?"

Ed now felt thoroughly sick to his stomach. It was hard enough asking himself this question ten thousand times a minute. It was even worse asking Gaia. But saying the answer out loud. . . having to hear the answer echo through this very large apartment and settle into Natasha's ears. . . . That was just sheer unadulterated agony—Ed's stock-in-trade for the last twenty-four hours. But there was, of course, only one answer.

"I don't know," he said with a simple shrug and a desperate smile. "I really don't know."

The room seemed unbelievably silent for a moment. A long painful moment. And then. . .

"Well, if you don't know," Natasha said, "then it is clear to me that Gaia has made a very large mistake, Ed."

Amen again, Natasha. Amen and hallelujah.

121

GEN HADN'T BEEN KIDDING WHEN

she'd said they would eat like queens. How could one eat like a queen in New York City for free? It could only be done after midnight, but it could be done. At least, when one was with Gen, it could. Apparently one of the great advantages of living in this rich folks' ghost town was that all the restaurants closed so early. This meant that all the overnight restaurant trash was available for much longer periods. Yes, trash. They ate trash. Of course, garbage wasn't Gaia's idea of a gourmet dinner, but Gen had introduced her to a whole new world. The world of gourmet garbage. Upper East Side garbage was better than most of the regular food on Eighth Street. Gen had taken Gaia on a tour of the absolute finest after-hours garbage the Upper East Side had to offer.

Their first course had come fresh out of the trash behind the kitchen of Kan-Pai, a sushi restaurant on Seventy-seventh and Third, where they'd thrown out whole buckets of perfectly good edamame, hijiki, and white rice. Then Gaia had followed Gen through a veritable obstacle course of ripped-open fences, fire escape ladders, and loose basement doors, until they'd arrived behind the kitchen of Bella Donna, one of the finer Italian establishments in the city. Gen showed Gaia the window that no one ever seemed to lock. It led straight into the kitchen. And even though Gaia wasn't a particular fan of breaking and entering, if the crime was simply taking some delicious homemade bread and dipping it in a scrumptious cold puttanesca sauce. . . then let her be guilty.

For dessert, Gen introduced Gaia to the Dumpster behind the Gardenia restaurant, where entire pies were discarded still in their boxes and most important. . . *boxes of doughnuts*. Gaia had chowed down on three just barely stale chocolate glazed doughnuts and then washed them down at six in the morning with free coffee provided by a vendor on Lexington Avenue whom Gen had obviously flirted into complete submission. All in all, though it had taken hours to complete the mission, it was the best meal Gaia had eaten in weeks, especially when combined with the thrill of the hunt.

Not to mention the good company. Not only was Gen funny and completely insane, but her similarities to Mary had made her more endearing to Gaia by the minute. Even the streak of red hair reminded her of Mary, though it was the fakest red Gaia had ever seen.

Gen and Mary shared a certain "screw them all" quality that seemed to bring Gaia to life. And considering how little of a life she had left, that was a much needed boost. It was something about their attitude. Gen had the same ability as Mary to get Gaia to do things she simply never would have done in a million years—namely, to have fun, to actually have *fun*. In fact, even Mary probably wouldn't have been able to get Gaia to eat doughnuts from a Dumpster. Even if they were in a box in the Dumpster. Even if they were chocolate glazed.

The only problem was the other very unfortunate similarity between them. All you had to do was change a few names. Heroin instead of cocaine. Casper instead of Skizz.

Skizz. Even thinking the name of Mary's dealer and murderer sent a flow of vengeful bile up Gaia's throat. She would have killed him if she'd had the chance. Unfortunately someone else had gotten to him first.

Gaia had worked hard to let go of all her poisonous anger toward Skizz. It had been eating up her insides for a very long time. And she'd been pretty sure she'd finally overcome it. she'd been pretty sure she'd moved on. But the minute she and Gen had started talking about Casper, all kinds of feelings had started to pop up again. Nagging memories of Skizz's ugly face—all the bitterness and rage she'd thought she'd flushed away.

"So Casper's your dealer?" Gaia asked, thinking about the first time she'd talked to Mary about Skizz.

They were walking back in the direction of the Seventy-second Street apartment, holding tight to their free coffees. The morning sun was blinding, especially after having stayed up all night foraging in the dark like a couple of urban not-so-chic raccoons.

Gen blew a puff of smoke into the air. "Sometimes

he's my dealer, sometimes he's my boyfriend," she said looking straight ahead. "It depends on how much money I have and how desperate I am for a fix."

Gaia cringed internally. Drug addiction made people do such disgusting things. She had no understanding of it whatsoever. Especially considering all that peripheral badness that came with it: dealers, overdoses, violence. What could possibly be the allure of that life? She'd asked that question a thousand times about Mary, and now she'd already found herself asking it about Gen when she barely even knew her. That was a bad sign. Caring too much already. Gaia couldn't forget about clause number three in her letter of resignation. *Don't get too close to anyone.*

"So was he your boyfriend last night when he was beating the shit out of you?" Gaia asked. Maybe not the friendliest way to phrase it, but she couldn't help herself. The whole "victim" aspect of addicts was so infuriating to her. Addicts were always making themselves somebody's victim, if not their own.

"Whatever," Gen scoffed "He gets violent sometimes. He thinks he's a real badass, but I can handle him."

"Like you handled him last night?" Gaia couldn't help saying.

"Okay, whatever." Gen groaned. "I already thanked you, didn't I? Don't worry about Casper. He's harmless."

"Harmless, huh?"

They walked a block in silence as Gaia tried her best

to hold her tongue from the next thing she wanted to say. But she was simply no good at holding her tongue. She wanted Gen to hear it. "You know, you kind of remind me of someone. She used to be my best friend, actually. She was addicted to coke. . . . She's dead now."

"I'm sorry to hear that," Gen said. "I know a lot of people who've OD'd on coke."

"She didn't OD," Gaia said. "She was killed by her dealer. You know. . . her *harmless* dealer." Okay. She'd said it. She'd made her point. Gen was silent for the next block. And Gaia didn't want to say any more. Her need to "save" Gen from the same fate as Mary Moss had just kind of snuck up on her, and the last thing she wanted to do was start a punishing just-say-no lecture. There was nothing worse than a condescending savior. She knew she'd probably taken it a little too far, and she braced herself for Gen to get pissed off.

"Well. . ." Gen sighed after a block and a half. "I guess you're just going to have to stick by me at all times, then." She turned to Gaia and smiled. "You can flip his Sugar Ray ass the next time he tries something."

Gaia tried not to smile too openly at the suggestion, but the truth was, Gen had just made her day. Protecting Gen from Casper. Maybe even helping her off the drugs—something, much to her shame, she'd been unable to do for Mary. This could be exactly what her new emptied-out life needed. She knew she wasn't supposed to get too close to anyone, but this wouldn't just be about being friends. This could also be some much needed karmic payback for letting Mary down. Besides, finding people to save uptown had been a real bitch, and Gaia had just been offered a permanent savior assignment. How can't she turn that down? "It would be my pleasure," she said, hoping it hadn't come out sounding too corny.

Gen ruffled Gaia's hair as though she were four years old, and that seemed to signal that the uncomfortable conversation was over. For some reason, coming from Gen, this condescending gesture didn't bother Gaia.

They didn't speak again until they'd arrived in front of Gaia's house, if you could even call it that, which she didn't particularly like to do. "This is it," Gaia said, stopping under the awning and turning away from the annoying uniformed doorman.

"*This* is where you live?" Gen uttered, peering through the glass doors into the embarrassingly ornate lobby.

"I don't really *live* here," Gaia assured her, looking at the entire building with disdain. "It's just where I'm staying."

"Well, who are you staying with?" Gen asked.

"I don't even know them."

"Huh. . . And your dad's not here?"

"*No*," Gaia said. "I already told you, I have no idea where he is. What is your obsession with my dad? *Oh, crap.*"

Gen spun back to Gaia. "What's wrong?"

"*Crap!*" Gaia whispered to herself again.

"What? What's your problem?"

Her problem was walking up the block. Two problems, actually, with coffees in their hands. And it was too late to make a quick escape. They'd already seen her. Ed was already calling out her name. And Tatiana was already giving her the evil eye.

SEEING ED'S FACE HAD BASICALLY braided Gaia's guts together. She just hadn't been prepared for it. *Don't even look at him,* she told herself.

Electrical Surge

The problem with looking at him was that it made her want to lean her head between his neck and shoulder and stay there for an indefinite period of time. She wanted to grab his hand, hail a cab, and go back to his bed for the next three days. Because that's really where they should be right now. They should be in bed. Not standing out in the relative cold, staring at each other like strangers.

Looking at Ed now felt exactly the same as looking at old pictures of her family from before her mother had died. It was like she could see her happy home just inches from her fingertips. Right in front of her was joy and safety and a future, and Gaia couldn't touch it. She couldn't go near it or get inside it. So she couldn't bear to look at it. She just wanted to slam the book of photos closed before her resolve started to crumble—before *she* started to crumble into pieces right there in front of Gen and Tatiana and her uniformed doorman. Because she knew Ed all too well. And if he saw a chink in her armor, if he saw through to the truth of what she was feeling, then he'd never let it go. He'd find some way to chisel away at the cracks until the truth came out, not even understanding that he'd only be screwing himself in the process.

So, cold was the order of the day. Cold as ice. Colder than she'd even been to him the last time. Cold enough and hard enough to make sure he didn't come back for more. As cold as the stare Tatiana was giving her and Gen.

"Where were you all night?" Ed demanded as he and Tatiana faced down Gaia and Gen under the awning of the building. "I came here to talk to you this morning. I don't even *know* how long I've been waiting." Ed turned to Tatiana. "How long?"

"At least an hour," Tatiana replied.

"At least an hour," Ed repeated to Gaia. "Sitting in your house, waiting for you. We finally went out for coffees."

Gaia rolled her eyes to Tatiana with pure disgust. She was sure Tatiana must have just *hated* being forced into morning coffee with Ed. She might as well have had the phrase "I have a crush on Ed" embroidered on all her perfect little Calvin Klein outfits. She was probably hoping Gaia would disappear every morning. Then she and Ed could have coffee together on a regular basis.

"Don't look at *me*," Tatiana complained, bouncing Gaia's disgust right back at her. "You are the one who disappears. You think I like watching my mother walk around our house with worrying?"

"Whatever," Gaia muttered.

"Whatever," Tatiana hissed in reply. Her English might be slow going, but she was a quick mimic when it came to insults.

"So where were you?" Ed repeated. "Tatiana said you never even came home last night."

"Not to worry," Gen said, stepping into the conversation. "She was with me."

Ed turned his demanding eyes from Gaia's face and stared at Gen with utter bewilderment. "Who the hell are *you*?"

"*Nice*," Gen responded, turning to Gaia. "Real nice. Who is this guy, your boyfriend?"

"No," Gaia breathed to the ground, avoiding Ed's eyes.

"Well, then, *who*?" Gen asked, giving Ed a look of utter indifference.

"Yes, who am I, Gaia?" Ed asked, trying once again to catch her eyes. "I think that's a damn good question. Maybe you'd like to *talk* to me about that?"

Must get out of here. Must get out of here now. Never mind being cold to him, just run. Run your ass off. "I got to get upstairs—"

"Don't," Ed snapped, holding Gaia's arm. "Don't do that. Talk to me."

Gaia shook her arm from his grip, though in truth, even his angry touch had sparked reminders of their night together. She couldn't believe it. Even now. Even in the pre-school hours of the morning, with no sleep to speak of, arguing on the street, she could *still feel that electrical surge* when Ed touched her. God. If that electricity could cut through all her enforced avoidance and bitterness, Gaia couldn't imagine what she'd be feeling if they were in bed together right now like they should have been.

Correction. You won't *imagine what that would feel like. You* will *get your ass upstairs now.*

Gaia turned to Gen. "I'm going."

"Do you want some company?" Gen asked.

"No, I'm just going to get some sleep."

"You're sure? I can totally hang out. I'd hate to leave you with these two."

"I'm sorry, *who* are you again?" Ed spat, staring at Gen with a combination of suspicion and disdain.

"That's funny," Gen shot back, "'Cause I still don't know who *you* are, either. I know you're *not* her boyfriend."

Ed turned back to Gaia. "Who is this girl?"

"She's a friend of mine," Gaia replied, "and that's it for the question-and-answer period. Good-bye."

"*I* know," Gen announced to Ed. "Why don't you go out with Ms. Stick-Up-Her-Ass Two Thousand and One over here? Then you can have little blond rich bitch babies in Prada diapers."

Tatiana eyed Gen with repulsion, muttering something back in Russian. Gaia didn't quite catch it. It was something about being "low class."

"What did she just say?" Gen yelled, leaning in toward Tatiana. "Why don't you try that in English, bitch?"

"Your friend, huh?" Ed said. "She's charming."

"Okay, whatever," Gen huffed, throwing up her hands and backing away. "Gaia, if these are your friends, I think I'm starting to get why your life sucks so bad."

"*She's* not my friend," Gaia explained, pointing at Tatiana.

"Well, that's a relief," Gen called back. "Tell you what, when you're done chilling with Princess Prissy Bitch and Joe Crutches, give me a page, okay? I'm outta here." She turned to Tatiana as she backed away. "Farewell, Princess Prissy Bitch! If you'd like some help learning English, why don't you give me a page, too?" Finally Gen disappeared behind the corner.

"Where the hell did you find *her*?" Ed asked.

"What? She's right," Gaia replied. "Tatiana should speak English around us." She gave Tatiana one last dirty look. "It might keep her honest."

"Gaia—" Ed began.

"In fact, why don't *you* try to teach her, Ed?" she interrupted, turning away as quickly as possible. "You two seem to be getting along *so well.*"

Gaia pushed through the door and prayed that Ed wouldn't follow her. Given the current amount of electricity between them, she simply couldn't take it anymore. And his new buddy status with Tatiana wasn't helping. She just needed to get upstairs and go to sleep for at least a few hours. And maybe when she woke up. . . through some kind of miracle. . . he'd hate her. Oh, how she wished for that right now.

THIS WAS NOT AT ALL THE CON-

Fiery Blip

frontation Ed had in mind. It was supposed to be just Gaia and him in a quiet room, sharing some much needed honesty. Not Gaia, Ed, Tatiana, and Gaia's horrible new friend filling the space with ridiculously adolescent insults. Whoever that girl was, Ed didn't trust her in the least. He'd taken a severe and instant dislike to her and hoped he'd never be subjected to her again.

He watched through the glass doors of the building as Gaia disappeared into the elevator. But that couldn't be it. That pittance of a conversation wasn't what Ed had traveled miles and waited hours for. Gaia's averted glances and minor insults had left him feeling emptier and less resolved than their last encounter. So she'd really left him with no other choice. He swallowed a very deep breath, bowed his head, and went in after her. Christ, he was a glutton for punishment.

"What are you doing?" Tatiana asked as she followed him into the long marble hallway.

"What does it look like I'm doing?" he replied, tapping repeatedly on the elevator button.

"Ed," Tatiana said slowly. "I. . . do not think she wants you to follow her."

"I think you're right," Ed answered, putting an end to that argument quickly. Tatiana was kind enough to bite her tongue for the rest of the elevator ride up, though Ed could tell his choice had somehow upset her. But that wasn't his problem to deal with right now.

The elevator opened onto the small hallway, and Tatiana was at least mature enough to unlock the door for Ed even if she didn't approve of his pride-swallowing behavior.

There was no way she could understand what Ed and Gaia had shared the night before last. And if she were ever lucky enough to have a night like that, then Ed was sure she would understand why he wouldn't give up so easily. In fact, if anything, Ed saw it this way: If Gaia was truly breaking up with him before they'd even started going out, then at the very least, a night as passionate as the one they'd shared deserved a breakup fight just as passionate. And Ed would be damned if he wasn't going to make that fight happen or else bring back Gaia's sanity trying.

He walked briskly through the spacious, sunlit living room, which he could only refer to now as "the waiting room." When he got to her door, he knocked twice and opened it without waiting for a response.

Gaia was sprawled out on her bed, fully clothed, looking nothing less than in pain. When she saw Ed walk through the door, he could see her practically flinch with displeasure as she jumped out of bed and walked to the other side of the room. "Ed. . ." she choked out as if she were at the end of her rope.

"Look," he said, keeping his distance. "The thing is. . . I got a call from the police yesterday, and they asked me if I'd come in and talk about the shooting, and I just thought. . . that you might go with me to the station this morning since you saw the whole thing go down."

"I can't," she said, standing with her back literally pressed against the wall. "I'm sorry, Ed, but. . . you've got to go."

Ed dropped his head in frustration at yet another failed attempt and considered his next move. Scream and yell? Quiet and gentle? Maybe he should just drop to his knees and plead for the real Gaia to return to him. But years of trying to be easygoing had left him stuck in the world of the reasonable. "Okay, do you think it's safe to say that there's something you're not telling me?"

Gaia kicked the sole of her foot against the wall. Her face became tighter and tighter, as if someone were slowly closing a vise on her head. Ed hadn't expected to feel so guilty about confronting her, but that's just how the pain on her face had begun to affect him. As if *he* should somehow feel guilty for torturing *her* in this scenario. There was a joke, if he'd ever heard one.

"Ed," she murmured, her voice simmering with all kinds of potential for explosion, "I *need* to get some sleep, okay? I've been up all night."

"It's just a trip to the police station, Gaia. It's not that big—"

"Ed, please!" she barked. "I'm sorry that I can't go, but I'm sure there were plenty of other witnesses."

Ed was quickly running out of reasonablness. "Do you even care that I could have been killed yesterday?"

"Of course I do!" she moaned. "Don't be ridiculous. And you have *no idea* how happy I am that you're okay, but you know what, Ed? You should be enjoying your life now that you've got it. You don't need to be around all my miserable crap."

"*Yes*," Ed spat out emphatically, "as a matter of fact,

I *do*. I *need* to be around your miserable crap every day, Gaia, and every night. I thought that's where we were headed. I thought that's what we'd gotten to. And then you dug *way down deep* and found an *even deeper* layer of miserable crap for me to contend with. I don't know how you did it, but you did, and you know what? I *still* need to be around it! That's the point of us, isn't it? That I love every ounce of your miserable crap."

"Please," she begged. "Just go!"

"Oh, come on." Ed groaned, slamming his fist on the doorway. "That speech was good! I just put that together right on the spot just now!"

"*Ed!*" she howled at a pitch high enough to buzz his eardrums. "Enough! I asked you to leave, now leave!"

Gaia kicked her wall again and then escaped her room, rushing past Ed into the living room. He followed her out, arguing, barely even registering that they were now putting on a full-fledged show for Tatiana, who was seated most uncomfortably on the living-room couch. Not to mention Natasha, who must have been respectfully hiding around the corner.

"I can't leave without some explanation," he barked. "Something *real*."

"I gave you an explanation. You just don't want to believe it's true."

"No, I don't!"

"Well, then why don't you get out of here and go mull it over. Because here's your news flash, Fargo. I

137

meant every word of it! Okay? Every goddamn word! I was just a basket case, and. . . and. . . I *needed* someone, and you were *there*. Okay? And that's it. It was just a mistake, Ed. A big mistake, and now I need to be alone for a while. Understood? Is that clear and honest enough for you? *Leave me alone.*"

Ed's entire body felt wobbly and bent backward. If she said one more cruel word, he probably would fall over. "And you won't even come with me to the police station?" he squeaked indignantly, not even knowing what else to say after her horrid little rant.

"No! I can't. I'm tired, and I'm going to bed!"

"I can go with you," Tatiana interjected from the couch.

Ed and Gaia both went silent as they turned to Tatiana. He had nearly forgotten she was sitting there. He was a bit mortified at having exposed her quite so mercilessly to his and Gaia's dirty laundry, but still, she had placed an offer on the table. And Gaia had slashed away so deeply at Ed's ego. . . that he felt compelled to accept it. Especially since Gaia was there to watch him accept it.

"Well, *thank you*, Tatiana," Ed crooned, shooting Gaia a vicious glance. "That's *very nice* of you. I could use the moral support." He stepped over to Tatiana and offered his hand to her as she rose from the couch. Then he turned back to Gaia, whose face had begun to turn a pale shade of red as she stared hatefully at Tatiana.

"Of course," Tatiana said with a wide smile.

"Well, there you go," Ed said with a deeply ironic happy grin on his face. "You can get some sleep now, Gaia, because Tatiana's going to come with me. Problem solved. I'm really glad we had this talk. And maybe Tatiana and I will see you later in school, okay? *Great!* See you later."

Gaia didn't utter another word as Ed politely escorted Tatiana to the door. He made sure Gaia watched as he smiled at Tatiana, placed his hand gently on her back, and escorted her out to the elevator. Then he turned back to Gaia and gave her one last look.

He wasn't even sure what this last look was for. He wasn't sure what it was meant to say. Some part of him was just so angry that he wanted to stay for one last vengeful moment, to rub Tatiana in her face. But mostly. . .

In spite of all Gaia's mind-blowing insensitivity and all the lacerating wounds she'd just inflicted on his ego, mostly. . . he just wanted another moment with her. Because the reality of the situation had finally cut through. He was sure now. This wasn't some kind of test or some kind of game she was playing. It wasn't just another one of Gaia's hyper-extreme hot and cold spells. And she had no secret agenda.

She simply didn't love him. That was the big secret. That was the all-important *truth* he'd been looking for. She'd been swirling around in the chaos of her life, and she'd gotten caught up in the heat of the moment with Ed. And that was all. That particularly well-heated moment was over.

So maybe his last look at her cold but troubled face was really just meant to say good-bye. Because he'd gotten what he came for. A loud and fiery breakup to go with their `fiery blip of a romance.`

All that was really left to do was slam the door closed. Which he did. As loud and as hard as he could.

In my country, if a woman were to treat a man as abominably as I have seen Gaia treat Ed, she would be placed on a horse backward, blindfolded, and sent out to the Siberian desert with a thimbleful of water.

Perhaps that's a bit of an exaggeration. But still, I simply can't believe the horrid way she treats Ed. It disgusts me.

The way she treats me is quite sickening as well, but at least we have no prior relationship. Ed is supposed to be her boyfriend. At least that's what she told *me* to my face. But if this is the way a girl treats her boyfriend in America, then this place is even more horrible than I thought. What kind of culture could possibly allow someone to be so cruel to a loved one? Unless, of course, he is not a loved one. Confusing. Very confusing.

Then there is the issue of her foul-mouthed orangutan of a friend.

I could say plenty of cruel things
about Gaia, which I will respectfully refrain from doing at this
moment, but she certainly strikes
me as intelligent. How could she be
so foolish as to place her trust in
that awful girl?

Indeed, my mother really has
yet to convince me of any of this
country's great advantages.
Although I suppose. . . Ed is
American. And I will admit that
he is kinder and funnier than any
boy I knew in Russia. And I suppose I would have to admit, more
attractive, too.

But contrary to what Gaia
might believe, I am *not* trying to
make some kind of immoral play
for his affections.

However, I think even Gaia would
admit that—*hypothetically,* of
course—if, for instance, we lived
in some kind of parallel universe
and Ed *were* to be my boyfriend. . .
that I would never treat him the
way she treats him. Never.

From: jbrown@alloymail.com
To: heatherg@alloymail.com
Time: 1:45 P.M.
Re: Starbucks sucks

Heather,

   Am I the only one who's getting a little tired of coffee?

   Here's what I'm thinking. In the immortal words of Emeril Lagasse, what do you say we kick things up a notch? Meet me at 9:00 at Guernica, 25 Avenue B.

   My hidden agenda: to see you in a party dress.

   But you probably already know that, what with your mind control and all.

                    Josh (your own personal voodoo doll)

From: heatherg@alloymail.com
To: jbrown@alloymail.com
Time: 3:42 P.M.
Re: Starbucks sucks

Josh,

   Yup. Already knew, already picked out the dress. Hope you like.

   See you there.

                    XOXO (if you're lucky)
                    Heather

With the
exception of
Adolf Hitler,
there was

unnecessary
flashbacks

no name she
despised more
than the name
Josh.

"TANGERINE OR *MANGO*? HEL-*LO*?"

Lack of Love

Heather's entire body shook with fear. Just the sheer volume of the voice of the kitchen worker in charge of Jell-O had shocked her awake. She'd been caught in her fourth Josh-induced love trance of the day, and she was really beginning to piss people off. In this case, it was an entire line of greasy-faced students dying to make that all-important decision of mango versus tangerine Jell-O, and Heather was apparently ruining their lives by holding up the line, stuck in a romantic fantasyland. She'd been reliving Josh's exquisite kiss on the cheek when she 'd been so rudely interrupted.

"Moooove," a scrawny sophomore with braces and a backward baseball cap hollered.

Heather turned to him and winced with disgust at his lack of manners. "What*ever*," she spat. "I'm not even *having* lunch today."

"Then *mooooove*."

"I'm *moving*."

Heather grabbed her empty tray from the line and put it straight into the stack of dirties. The smile quickly returned to her face, though. Nothing could bother her today. After all, how could that hopeless young twig be expected to understand? What did he know about true love in his young life? He would surely be at home tonight, trying to choose between his Dreamcast and his Xbox, while Heather was at Guernica being swept just that much further off her feet by an honest-to-goodness *man*.

Thoughts of her date tonight were averaging about one every fifteen seconds, culminating in a completely frozen love trance about once an hour. During the course of the day, this compromised state of awareness had caused her to block the locker of one freshman girl who'd been too intimidated to say anything, to create a bottleneck situation on the stairs during a fire drill, and to blank on three straight questions during astronomy. So impaired was her judgment that she'd even been tempted to try and explain her situation to her teacher, woman to woman.

Look, Ms. Etchison, she would have said, *you and I know both know there are things in this life far more important than population 1 and 2 stars. There is love and there is passion, and there is that moment when the hottest guy in the world wants to see you in your party dress. Do you remember that moment, Ms. Etchison? Well. . . you probably never had that moment, but still. . . isn't that what the stars are really for, Ms. Etchison? After all is said and done, aren't the stars really made for Josh Brown and me? To stare at tonight after the club? To talk about in our prekiss banter about constellations? Haven't you ever heard the term "star-crossed lovers"? I don't know what it means, Ms. Etchison, but I know it's about lovers and stars, so it must be about Josh Brown and me.*

Heather had opted not to give her speech, simply because it would have taken too long, but still, it was true. There were things in this world so much more important than astronomy. This world of school and cafeterias and greasy-faced students had come to seem so unbelievably *small*. Heather would never have shared this particular choice of words openly, but in all honesty, after spending time with Josh, she couldn't help feeling that this whole high school thing was just a tad beneath her.

Still, even though her friends had all gone out for sushi, Heather had opted for the cafeteria. Why? Because maybe. . . just perhaps. . . she might want to run into Ed and Gaia. And maybe, perhaps, she thought they might be interested to know that her Starbucks crush had turned into something far more substantial. Something perhaps even to rival their all-powerful romance. Yes, she thought they just might like to know that.

Heather finally saw Ed's wild hair in a corner of the cafeteria and headed for his table. She could only see the back of Gaia's head, but it was quite obvious that they were having some very serious and intimate private conversation. Perfect time to pay them a little visit.

New leaf, Heather. Don't forget about your new leaf.

Heather tried to focus on her new leaf for a moment. But today she couldn't help wondering. . .

What the hell was the point of the new leaf? What was the point of trying to be more giving when the people you were trying to give to weren't even taking? Ed and Gaia had just started their big whirlwind relationship; they honestly didn't seem to care whether Heather was being unselfish or not. And a few resentful barbs thrown in their direction? Was that really such a crime? Ed had flat out dumped Heather. And then he'd started up with Gaia maybe a week or so later. It wasn't like Heather hadn't seen what was going on. Ed had been pining for his "best friend" for months, and once she'd finally come around, Heather had been history. So didn't she really have the right to be a tad resentful? Wasn't that just a valid and honest response?

Honesty. That was the main thing Heather was really starting to learn about from Josh. Being honest with herself had finally begun to bring back some of her confidence. After coping with her sister's battle with anorexia, her family's sudden financial problems, and losing both Sam *and* Ed to Gaia, her confidence had pretty much hit rock bottom. But Josh was changing all that. He'd reminded Heather who she was, and now she wanted to remind a few other people as well.

Not that a turning over a new leaf wasn't a beautiful thing, but in all honesty. . . spring couldn't last forever.

"What's up, lovebirds?" Heather began as she pulled up to Ed and Gaia. Only when she took a closer look, she realized it wasn't Gaia. All she'd seen as she approached was the blond hair, and now she realized it was Gaia's new friend Tatiana sharing this very serious moment with Ed. Heather already felt somewhat unwelcome at the table, but she was simply in too good a mood to care.

"What's up," Ed uttered in a monotone.

"Sorry about the 'lovebirds' thing," Heather said as she swooped into a chair next to them. "You two just seemed so *cozy*."

Tatiana smiled shyly as she looked back at Ed. Ed stared down at his fork.

"Where's Gaia?" Heather asked. The question seemed to weigh their faces down even further.

"Don't know," Ed mumbled, digging back into his food with his eyes on the table. "We just got here."

"To school?" Heather asked.

"Yeah."

"*We. . . ?* As in. . . you and Tatiana?"

This question didn't seem to warrant a response, in Ed's opinion. Heather had never seen two people become more focused on their institutional lunches. "Well, where were you two?"

Tatiana shared a silent glance with Ed as if he was supposed to field the question.

"Doctor," he said finally. "Tatiana came with me to the doctor."

"Well, isn't that nice." Heather smiled, racking her

brains for what might really be going on. "Why didn't Gaia go with you?"

Another question Ed didn't seem to deem worth answering. The plot thickened.

"Well, how are you?" Heather tried.

"What do you mean?" Ed replied defensively, looking up quickly from his meal.

Heather's eyes widened at his prickly response. "The doctor...," she said timidly. "How did it go?"

"Oh," Ed grunted. "Fine, it was fine." Back to his food. Heather waited for Ed to supply a polite response, but given his particularly ornery state, she realized she'd need to do the work for him.

"Well, ask me how I am," she said with a smile.

Ed looked up at her with a cold, disinterested stare. He seemed to be debating whether he'd even honor her request. But Heather was prepared to wait as long as it took. "How are you?" he finally asked sarcastically, making it clear that he'd been coerced.

"I am ridiculously, amazingly *wonderful*," she replied, picking a grape off Ed's tray.

Tatiana smiled at her. Ed turned back to his tray. "That's good," he muttered.

"Ask me why," Heather prompted him.

"Why." Ed sighed.

"Because I'm head over heels in love!" she announced finally with her largest grin.

"Coffee-in-the-lap guy?" Ed muttered with disinterest

as he bit into his sandwich. This was not the response she was after.

"*Yes*, but he's so much more than that. Josh is like this. . ."

Ed began to loudly unwrap his brownie. There just wasn't an ounce of jealousy in him. He wasn't even listening. "Oh, you're no fun," she said, slapping him on the shoulder. If Heather hadn't moved on to a far superior man, she would have been deeply hurt right now. Lack of jealousy equals lack of love, respect, and admiration. But instead she just looked at her former boyfriend, wondering when he'd turned into such a sour and mopey individual. Though the answer was obvious. It was right around the time he'd begun a relationship with a certain sour and mopey blond. A mopey blond who just happened to make a rare appearance in the cafeteria at that very moment.

"Well, there she is!" Heather squealed, pointing to Gaia at the food line, watching as she grabbed a tray and slammed it down on the counter. Perhaps Gaia would be more receptive to envy-inducing tales of Heather's new love life. In a way, Heather almost wanted Gaia to know of her good fortune even more than Ed. Especially now that telling Ed had proved to be such a thoroughly dissatisfying experience. "Ed. . ." She waved her hand in Ed's unresponsive face. "Ed, your woman has arrived," she said, waiting for him to jump out of his chair or at least call to her. . . . No response.

"Ed. . . ?" she tried again, watching him munch on his food with no expression. "*Ed—*"

"Yeah, I *saw* her," Ed snapped, giving Heather a surprisingly harsh glance. "Thanks. I've got it. She's here."

This was getting stranger by the second. And far more intriguing. "Well, I'll go get her!" Heather volunteered enthusiastically as she shot out of her chair.

"That's not necessary," Ed called to her as she headed for the food line.

"Oh, but it is," Heather called back. "I really think it is."

"GAIA!"

Gaia slammed her eyes shut the second she heard Heather's high-pitched squeal. Why wasn't she at sushi with  the FOHs? The coast was supposed to be clear—that was the entire point. She'd *known* the cafeteria would be a mistake; she'd just thought she could get in and out before she'd have to deal with anyone. Stupid. Really stupid.

"Gaia!" Heather called again as she pulled up next to her in line. "What's *up,* girl?"

Gaia tried to focus on her Jell-O choices and ignore

Heather. "Absolutely nothing," she said. Translation: *Please, please go away.*

"Cool," Heather replied with the utmost obliviousness. She obviously didn't speak Gaia. "How *are* you, girl?"

When exactly had Gaia become Heather's "girl?"

"I'm fine," Gaia replied, examining the rotting fruit options.

"Ask me how I am," Heather insisted gleefully, rocking back and forth at the counter.

"How are you?" Gaia repeated back with the emotion of an android.

"I'm *awesome!*" Heather squealed yet again. "Ask me why."

"Why?"

"Because I'm in *love,* that's why!" Heather began to perform a most unfortunate dance around Gaia as she tried to grab some soda. "I'm in love, I'm in love, I'm in love," she sang quietly.

Gaia feared she might grind her teeth down to dust if this were to continue. Two things she really couldn't deal with right now: Heather Gannis. . . and love. "Congrats," she muttered, at least trying to get Heather to stop singing. "Coffee-in-the-lap guy?"

"Yes, but he's got a *name* now."

"What's his name?"

"*Josh.*" Heather sighed. "Isn't that a perfect name?"

Gaia nearly dropped her tray on a student's head

when she heard that horrific name. Acid began to painfully burn at the base of her throat.

With the exception of Adolf Hitler, there was no name she despised more than the name Josh. But it couldn't possibly be *the* Josh. That could only be the remains of Gaia's fearful, paranoid feelings from her uncle's injection. After all, there were still traces of fear from whatever he'd given her; why shouldn't there be traces of paranoia? That's what it had to be. Because what could *they* possibly want with Heather Gannis? It couldn't possibly be that Gaia had gotten "too close" to Heather, nor could Gaia imagine any particular purpose that Heather could serve Loki.

You're being ridiculous, she told herself. *There are eight million Joshes in this naked city, and you only know one of them.* Well. . . actually *three* of them would be more accurate if she counted Josh's clones—his "qualified replicants" as it were. What were the odds it was the same one? And even if it were, what could she possibly say to Heather about it?

I know a guy named Josh. He's got two clones of himself, and they all work for my uncle or my father. They've been trying to terrorize me for months now, and they've already killed Sam. Oh, yeah, Heather, by the way, Sam is dead and it's my fault. But it might not be the same Josh. . . .

Paranoid. Definitely paranoid. Gaia did everything in her power to shake Josh from her mind and find a place to eat her Jell-O. "Great name," she said. The only answer was to humor Heather.

"Well, I want to tell you all about him," Heather said. "Come on, we're over by the front tables."

Gaia followed Heather blindly until she realized exactly who was at the front tables.

They were supposed to be at the police station. This is a goddamn ambush.

Heather and the FOHs were supposed to be at sushi, and Ed and Tatiana were supposed to be at the police station, thus her choice of the cafeteria. A choice that was increasingly proving to be a massive error on Gaia's part.

"You know what?" Gaia said, beginning a slow retreat in the other direction. "I just stopped in for a quick bite, and then I've really got to get to a class. No real time to talk."

She scanned the room for another table and found a reasonably empty one to the side, where she quickly pulled in and slammed down her tray.

Heather stayed rooted to the ground, staring with bewilderment as Gaia took a seat and spooned herself a large glob of repulsive mango Jell-O. Once Gaia had ignored Heather's confused glances for long enough, Heather finally walked over to her table and sat down across from her. This was *not* what Gaia had hoped would happen.

"Okay, what's going on?" she whispered excitedly,

as if they were on some E! Entertainment gossip show.

"What are you talking about?" Gaia mumbled through her Jell-O, wondering how quickly she could finish it.

"Oh, come on," Heather said. "Do I detect some trouble in paradise or what?"

Could she have been any more excited if she had?

"I don't know what you're talking about," Gaia mumbled.

"*Gaia,*" she moaned. "Here. Look at my face." She grinned enormously from ear to ear. "That's what a person in love looks like. Now look at your face and Ed's face, and tell me that nothing's wrong."

Gaia completely ignored Heather's suggestion and focused entirely on the remains of her wobbly Jell-O instead.

"Well, then, look at *them,*" Heather insisted, leaning in with a strained whisper. "At least tell me what *that's* all about."

Gaia dropped her spoon into the bowl and glared at Heather. Why did she have to do this? Why did she have to throw this in Gaia's face right now? Wasn't it bad enough that Gaia had been ambushed? Wasn't it bad enough that she'd had to listen to Heather call her "girl?" That she'd had to listen to her *sing?* About *love,* no less. That she'd had to hear the name Josh tossed around, causing all kinds of `horrific unnecessary flashbacks`? Now Heather was going to force her to look at the one thing in this world that could still actually cause her pain?

Fine. Fine, she was going to have to get used to it, anyway. She was going to have to get used to seeing him and feeling nothing. That was the mandatory goal, and it was never going to get any easier. Why not start today? Gaia gave Heather one last filthy look, took a deep breath, and turned around.

Her heart broke as she watched Ed staring down at his tray, looking absolutely sullen. Tatiana reached her hand across the table and gave Ed's forehead a little poke. When he raised his eyes to her, she gave him a sweet, sympathetic smile, and Ed mustered a kind and appreciative grin in return.

How *sweet*. How very *adorable*. How absolutely and completely sickening and unbearable to watch. Gaia felt her heart drop out from under her as her entire body went hollow. It was even more agonizing to watch than it had been this morning. Because this time it wasn't even for Gaia's benefit. It was just happening. Gaia had spent the last twenty-four hours doing everything in her power to kick Ed into Tatiana's arms, and there was Tatiana, crouched low to the ground with her net, ready and waiting to catch him. How very generous of her. How very disgustingly kind.

Gaia could feel her entire body flooding with a deep, primal hatred for Tatiana. Suddenly every single aspect of her was infuriating, from her ludicrously silky blond hair, to her slim little nose, down to her elegant little waifish body, culminating in her coy and cuddly little you've-got-a-friend smile. Gen had really hit it on the nose. She'd gotten the whole picture in one two-minute meeting. *Princess Prissy Bitch. All hail.*

Ed suddenly turned toward Gaia. He had caught her completely off guard, leaving her no chance to cast the appropriate coldness over her face. He must have caught a glimpse of every ounce of pain, resentment, and loss in her eyes, because she could sense his eyes begin to search hers for their connection again. And if she didn't look away immediately, he was going to find it—he would have looked at just the right moment to see the truth: that shunning him felt like a slow suicide and losing him to Princess Prissy Bitch was like medieval torture.

Turn away, Gaia. Turn away and get out. Think about Sam. Think about what happened to Sam.

With every ounce of her will, Gaia dropped an ax on their near reconnection, turning back around to Heather and leaving Ed nothing but the back of her head to look at. But Heather's idiot grin was no better a sight, and it became immediately apparent to Gaia that school, and all the people in it, posed an entirely untenable situation, at least for today.

Without a word or even another glance in anyone's direction, Gaia shot out of her chair, launched herself through the rusty swinging doors of the cafeteria, and stumbled her way to the pay phone at the end of the hall. As she reached for the dial pad, she was able to recall Gen's pager number instantly. At least whatever Oliver had put in that crazy injection hadn't messed with her photographic memory.

Gaia was in dire need of an escape. An escape from this world of BS artists, *herself* now very much included. An escape from the whole two-faced world of girls like Tatiana and Heather. And Natasha, too. Makeup and pretty faces to cover their scheming little eyes. She had to see Gen. The one girl she knew who wasn't full of crap—the one girl who, near as she could tell, didn't have a hidden agenda.

Memo

From: G

To: L

Subject is approaching abandoned boathouse near the pond in Central Park. Awaiting instructions.

Memo

From: L

To: G

Stick to the prime directives. Get as close as possible. Gather as much info as possible. Report all pertinent details.

"WAIT, I'M CONFUSED," GEN COM-
plained. "Joe Crutches *is* your boy-friend, or he isn't? Which one is it?"

In Cold Blood

Gen and Gaia were lying on either side of a dusty wooden rowboat in the old abandoned boathouse next to the Central Park pond. It was a wide, spacious shack. There were a couple more dead wooden boats stacked on the ground, and there was one large old sailboat hanging by thick braided ropes from the ceiling. Piles of dusty, splintered oars littered the corner, and a few cases of obsolete life jackets sat under the window. Everything was covered either in rust or in thick green paint, but you couldn't beat it for privacy. Of course, Gen had known how to shove open one of the old windows so they could climb in and step down off the piles of life jackets.

Gaia had been looking forward to some confessional conversation, but she'd neglected to consider just how complicated any honest explanation of her life would be. She kept trying to give Gen the short version, but it wasn't translating very well.

"Well, he isn't my boyfriend, but even if he isn't my boyfriend. . ."

"Princess Prissy Bitch is still a bitch," Gen said, finishing Gaia's sentence.

"*Exactly.*" Gaia laughed. "I mean, even if Ed and I—and his name is *Ed,* by the way. Not Joe Crutches. I'm all for 'Princess Prissy Bitch,' but that 'Joe Crutches' thing has got to go."

"That's cool," Gen agreed.

"Anyway," Gaia went on, staring up at the cobwebs on the hanging sailboat, "I swear, even if Ed *were* my boyfriend, I think she'd be trying to move in on him. I mean, she's just shady. I don't trust her. I wouldn't trust her any further than I could throw. . . Well, actually I could throw her pretty far."

"I know, right?" Gen howled with laughter. "That chick's like a little blond javelin or something. That should be some kind of Olympic event. The Princess Prissy Bitch toss. I think I could capture the silver on that one." They gave in to a contagious laughing fit until the laughs finally began to die down.

Gaia was extremely glad she'd called Gen. It had definitely been the right choice. She hadn't felt this comfortable bitching with someone since Mary, and bitching was, of course, a natural and necessary part of human existence. Ed had always tried to be a decent bitching partner (a memory Gaia quickly had to block from her head), but there was still a kind of communication that could really only take place between two girls. Gaia hadn't even realized how much she'd missed it until she'd met Gen.

Unfortunately, the more Gaia's thoughts swayed toward memories of Mary, the more she began to focus again on the problems Mary and Gen shared. The problems that Gaia had committed herself to solving.

"So here's what I was thinking...," Gaia announced.

"Uh-oh," Gen complained. "Here we go."

"No, come on, just hear me out. My friend Mary once told me about this... you know... some program that she went to somewhere upstate. She said it was like living in a goddamn country club. Three meals a day, sauna, gym. It was like—"

"*Gaia,*" Gen interrupted. "Come on, now. I already asked you to be my bodyguard. You don't need to be my drug counselor, too."

"Well, as your bodyguard," Gaia said, "your safety and well-being are my prime directives. And I happen to believe that if you were off the stuff, then you wouldn't have to deal with scumbags like Casper, that's all."

"We really don't have to worry about Casper," Gen reiterated. "The guy's a punk."

Gaia could literally hear Mary's voice in her head, saying the exact same thing about Skizz. "Don't worry about Skizz. The guy's a punk. I can handle Skizz." That was the one drawback to being a ballsy girl with attitude like Mary or Gen. They were so confident, they never even knew when they were in over their heads. It was a problem Gaia knew a little something about.

She sat up in the dusty boat and looked down at Gen. "Look, you're obviously very smart," she said with a sudden shift to extreme seriousness, "but on this

Casper issue. . . you don't know what you're talking about. Trust me, I've seen this go down before."

"Okay, chill." Gen smiled, basically blowing her off again.

"No, I'm serious!" Gaia snapped. "I'm *telling* you. This Casper guy is going to do something *bad*, Gen. I can feel it."

"Boo!" a voice hollered from the window.

Gaia shut her eyes in frustration, knowing instantly who it was before he'd even pushed his greasy, platinum-streaked head through the window. He'd probably been outside listening to Gaia's warning, just waiting to make the most dramatic entrance he could. Though "boo" didn't exactly qualify as dramatic in Gaia's book. And while she might be having some confusing issues with fear and paranoia, she was, thankfully, still quite impervious to "boo" as an effective means of terror. It could, however, elicit quick and overwhelming amounts of hatred.

One by one, Casper and his two thick, leather-clad thugs climbed through the boathouse window and landed their feet on the floor with a thud. This secluded spot was obviously a hideaway for both Gen *and* Casper. As Gaia's eyes drifted down to the rowboat she was sitting in, she wondered what Gen and Casper might have done in there. She leaped out of it with disgust, wiping the dust off her clothes. Gen just let out a frustrated sigh. She and Gaia both knew there was no other way out but that window.

"Don't be scared." Casper smiled as he approached them. "It's just the friendly ghost."

"He loves the whole friendly ghost thing." Gen groaned, rolling her eyes as she climbed out of the boat. "He thinks it's real clever."

"For him, it probably is," Gaia replied, crossing her arms. She fixed her eyes on Casper. "Don't worry," she said, staring him down, "in spite of your hair, we're still not afraid."

Casper let out a loud fake laugh, attempting to indicate that he could take a joke. He stepped much closer to Gaia, looked her up and down, and then breathed out a faint insulting laugh. "You know they make this shit that can make you look like a *girl* now? It's called *makeup*—look into it."

He and his friends shared a huge laugh, slapping hands before he stepped back in her face. "We've been looking for you," he said, his words nearly drowning in his Brooklyn accent. Gaia noticed for the first time that his rather large nose swerved over to the right side. "'Cause that shit you pulled last night. . . I mean, those self-defense classes definitely paid off, and you should be real proud—'grrl power' and all that shit" —he laughed, making air quotes with his fingers— "but you know, you really hurt my friend." He pointed back to the thug on his right, who'd apparently recovered from his run-in with his friend's knife.

"Gee, I'm sorry," Gaia said. "I was so busy trying not

to get stabbed, I wasn't thinking enough about your friend."

"Yeah, well, we don't have to worry about anyone getting cut again." Casper smiled, stepping far too close to Gaia. "*Psst,*" he whispered to her, motioning down toward his waist. Gaia looked down as he pulled a .38-caliber gun out of his pants and jabbed it into her stomach. "There. . . how's that feel?" he asked with a disgusting, lascivious moan. And then, as though performing a well-choreographed dance routine, his friends both pulled out their .38s in perfect unison.

Amazingly, Gaia's fearlike symptoms hadn't kicked in yet. She hoped perhaps that the remnants of her uncle's injection had finally left her system, but she did have an alternate theory. It was also quite possible that any fearful feelings she might have had were being over-powered completely by the swirling, rocking, thunder-ous `tropical storm of rage` that had just kicked up inside her chest as she looked in Casper's eyes.

Because at this point, Casper's face had all but disappeared, along with his voice. All that Gaia could see now was Skizz. All she could *hear* now was Skizz. Skizz's voice, Skizz's face, Skizz's gun pressed to the very spot where he'd shot Mary Moss and left her for dead.

"Cas, leave her alone," Gen insisted.

He whipped up the gun and placed it right between Gen's eyes. "*You,* I will deal with in a second.

Because *you're* the one that sicced this bitch on me in the first place. But first things first."

He jabbed the gun back into Gaia's stomach, leaning his disgusting Guido face even closer to hers. "So what do you think, bitch?" he whispered. "That is your name, right? Bitch? What do you think you could do to convince me not to pull this trigger right now?"

With the gun digging straight into her gut, there was still no room to maneuver. And he was going to shoot. A `misogynist asshole` like him who'd swung his knife at her with no hesitation? Who'd just gotten beaten up by a *girl* and was looking for payback? Yeah. He was going to shoot. No question about it. *Think, Gaia. You've got to remove the guns from the scenario, and you've got to do it fast.*

"Casper, come on," Gen said, her voice losing its usual confidence. "Don't do this, okay?"

"I told you," he shouted, "we talk after this is done."

Don't get involved, Gen, let me deal with this. I just need time to think.

"Whatever," Gen argued nervously. "She's scared, all right? You scared her. Congratulations, tough guy."

Casper shoved Gaia out of the way, dug his fingers into Gen's tattered sweater, and pulled her up to his face, cramming the gun into her stomach with a repulsive sneer.

No. Back to me. Get away from Gen and come back to me.

One of his thugs stepped next to Gaia, poking his gun to her right temple to hold her still.

"You want to start with the attitude again?" Casper shouted in Gen's ear. "You want to start that screaming shit you pulled last night when we were supposed to be having a good time?"

"A good time?" Gen squawked. "Is *that* what you call it when you put your greasy hands all over me? A 'good time?'"

"Oh, now you don't like the way I do it? Is that what you want this bitch to believe?"

"Gen, just leave it alone—" Gaia warned. But as per usual, Gen wasn't listening.

"Well, I wouldn't call it *a good time*, that's for sure." She laughed in his face.

"Oh, is that right? What would you call it?"

"I'd call it 'scoring drugs for free,' that's what I'd call it."

Gaia caught a glimpse of Casper's vicious glance before he brought his left arm back and slapped Gen so hard across the face that her entire body collapsed to the floor.

No. The moment his palm collided with her cheek, Gaia felt her entire body ignite. It was as though she could feel the slap herself. She could feel Casper's pathetic little hand lashing out across her cheek, stinging her eye, sending her down to the floor in a heap.

Gaia bit down on her tongue, replaying the slap again

and again in her head as her blood started burning. Each time she replayed it, there was less and less Gen and Casper, and more and more Mary and Skizz, until they were all she could see. Just Skizz standing there again with a satisfied grin, while Mary lay dead in a heap on the floor.

Gen jumped up and made a break for the window. "Gaia, run!" she screamed, launching her body through the window. "He won't shoot, just run!"

One of Casper's thugs made a move toward Gen, but Casper called him off. "Let her go," he ordered. "Where the hell is she gonna go? She lives in this freakin' park, junkie *bitch*." Gen made it through the window and ran as Casper turned back to Gaia. "We've still got what we came for." He smiled at Gaia, inching closer and closer, waving his gun, while his pathetic henchmen stood on either side of her, holding a gun to either side of her face.

They obviously had no idea how stupidly they'd arranged themselves. One of the first rules of gunplay: Never sandwich a target. Gaia had already forgotten about them. It was Casper she was focusing on. Or more specifically, Casper's body and Skizz's face.

She could taste her own blood leaking from her bitten tongue, and she couldn't help noticing how appropriate that was. Because once she'd witnessed that slap, the majority of her civility had melted away. It was as if her pupils had dilated and her claws had extended. She was out for blood now. She could literally taste it. Casper probably thought he was stalking *her* as he took each menacing step toward her, waving his little gun. But in actuality. . . Gaia was now stalking *him*. Just waiting for the right moment. . .

Just move a little closer. . . A little closer, you disgusting rapist misogynist asshole.

"Now, I can't decide," Casper said, leaning closer to her. "What should we start with? I mean, should we start with a kiss? Or should I just shove this gun in your mouth?"

She should have been supremely repulsed by his suggestion, but she was too busy reveling in the familiar fizz of prebattle concentration. If there was any fear or paranoia still running through her system, it had taken a much needed hiatus at this moment.

A kiss. What a perfect suggestion. That would bring him close enough for sure. "Kiss," Gaia uttered, drawing a mental *x* on the center of his forehead.

"Yeah, I thought you might say that." He smiled. He jabbed the gun in her stomach again and leaned forward.

As Casper leaned closer, Gaia leaned her head back.

"What are you doing?" he complained. "Don't you get scared on me, now."

Perfect. Don't move. Stay right there. "Actually, I'm not scared," she said, leaning her head back just a tad farther. "I just like precision."

Gaia launched her head forward like a slingshot, connecting dead center with the front of Casper's head. His head snapped back like a crash test dummy's as his whole body flew back about three feet, landing with an ear-shattering collision in the pile of old wooden oars. A split second after the vicious head butt, she immediately ducked low to the ground as the two meatheads fired off their guns in a panic, shooting bullets into each other's shoulders at practically point-blank range, sending them both flailing back and to the ground. Maybe now they'd learn never to sandwich a target.

With all three completely out of commission, Gaia leaped forward, snagging Casper's gun from the floor and rolling toward him, popping up right over his sprawled-out body. She reached down and grabbed his collar, making sure to snag as much chest hair as possible as she lodged the barrel of the gun deep into his mouth.

"Auugh!" he whimpered, flailing his arms with a look of absolute terror in his eyes. "Auugh." That was what the word *no* sounded like with a gun in your mouth.

Gaia could feel every ounce of predatory aggression coursing through her veins. She had never in her life killed a man in anything other than pure self-defense. Certainly not in cold blood. It went against every lesson in the *Go Rin No Sho*. It went against every ounce of her inherent morality. But this absolute waste of human tissue, this platinum-streaked, leather-clad troglodyte. . . he wasn't really a *man* per se. He was more of a *species*. A species of Skizzes and CJs.

Human impediments. That was their sole purpose in life. To make it impossible for people to move forward in their lives—to recover lives they might have lost along the way or lives they didn't even know they were entitled to living. It was really no different than what Loki had done to her. As long as Loki was alive, Gaia would be forced to continue her life sentence without the possibility for contentment or normalcy. And that was precisely the case with all the Skizzes and Caspers of the world. As long as they existed, the Marys and Gens of the world never really stood a chance. It was a most convincing argument for the complete extinction of this particular species.

With these thoughts coursing so strongly and definitely in her head, she found her thumb pulling back on the hammer of the gun and driving the barrel that much deeper down his throat.

"Auugh," he cried again much more urgently, pushing his hands uselessly against her shoulders as she held him to the ground. "Auugh." She wondered how many women had pushed against his shoulders crying "no" with utter futility. Certainly enough to justify ending his pathetic life. He shouldn't be living. There was no reason for him to live. Her index finger caressed the trigger and began to squeeze....

But she wasn't going to kill him. Because unfortunately, she wasn't a murderer. She just wanted to be sure he was listening.

"Listen to me now," she ordered, "because we are going to make an agreement."

"Ehggh," he replied with a desperate nod. That was "yes" with a gun in your mouth.

"You will *never,* I repeat, *never* go near Gen again, do you understand? You will leave this park, and you will leave this city, and you will *never* again put your freaking hands on a woman. And you will never again sell drugs to another human being. Do you understand my conditions?"

"Ehggh," he uttered, nodding emphatically.

"If you break any of these conditions," she said, "I will not hesitate to kill you. I made that mistake once before, and believe me, I will *not* make it again. And keep in mind. . ." She turned behind her and fired off two quick shots, severing each braided rope from about fifteen feet away, sending the sailboat that had been hanging from the ceiling falling to the ground. It landed directly on top of his two wounded buddies as she turned back to him. "I have very good aim."

She popped the barrel of the gun and let the bullets spill out, stepping over Casper's body as she crammed the gun in the back of her jeans. One quick step on the life jackets and she was through the window, back in the deceptively idyllic fields of Central

Park. She called out for Gen a few times, but she was obviously long gone. Which was a real shame. Gaia was very anxious to tell her the news: that she'd just been given the very thing that Mary Moss would never have. A second chance.

Gaia didn't
want to know
what kind of
crap her freaky

adrenaline

fake mom was up
to every **button**
night—strip
clubs? Late
night bingo?

HEATHER HAD BEEN INSECURE ABOUT
almost every aspect of her life
at one point or another. With
the exception of her appearance. Her beauty was the one
thing that had seemed almost
universally irrefutable. Whether
at school, at camp, on a bike

Fishnet Stockings

trip through Europe, even a day of community ser-
vice, it was always clear within the first three minutes
that she would be ranked, if not number one, then at
least in the top three of any female population. Even
the people who hated her most had never suggested
that she wasn't attractive.

This rare bit of unshakable security also carried
over to her taste—her ability to pick the outfit that
simply *worked*, that couldn't be faulted even by insecure competitive women or fashion-concious gay men.

But tonight. . . God help her, she just wasn't sure.
That was the awe-inspiring power of Josh Brown.

She'd e-mailed him that she had already picked out
her dress, when of course that wasn't true. How could
it be true? Only in preparing for this date had she realized how many variations on a black dress she had
amassed in just the last two seasons. And with the
exception of the two totally unrevealing ones (for
funerals and one-on-one dinners with her father) she
had tried on every single one.

Ultimately, after much very serious consideration, she had decided that this very important evening called for something just a little more than sexy. Tonight Heather had decided to go just a wee bit. . . trashy. A risky choice, yes. It wouldn't be right for just any occasion, but her instincts had never failed her before.

A full-force minidress. That was the decision. Low-cut top, formfitting middle, hanging just below the butt. And for sex kitten flavor. . . fishnet stockings. Classic, yet bold. But was she sure? This was what she'd been debating for the last five minutes after ducking into the ladies' room at Guernica before she'd even sat down to dinner. Was she absolutely sure it was the right choice? Would it turn him on without losing her an ounce of his respect?

Only his reaction could answer that question. That was how bad it had gotten. That was her degree of security when it came to Josh.

She applied one last lipstick touch-up, flipped around for one quick visible panty-line check, and that was that. She'd made her choices. She'd done all she could do. The rest was in the hands of fate. . . and Josh Brown. She finally tore herself away from the mirror and headed out to receive her score.

Guernica was small, but it was chock-full of undeniably cool people creating a din of hyperanimated urban cultural conversation. All the waiters' trays were overloaded with cosmopolitans and various martinis, and there was a general rumble of funk and soul music coming from the bar/dance floor downstairs. Heather's heart had begun racing halfway down Third Street, but by now she could almost hear it pounding as she searched between the thick crowd of shoulders and hairstyles for signs of Josh—as in spiky black hair, a pair of neon blue eyes, or a smile that seemed to have a life of its own.

And three tables in, sitting at a table for two against the wall that led to the kitchen, he finally appeared to her, his perfectly sculpted face lit up by warm golden candlelight as he sipped a glass of amber beer.

She wondered for a moment if *he* had maybe felt it necessary to take a little extra time in the mirror tonight. Maybe a little extra gel on the sides or perhaps the testing out of several shirts. But just observing the way he sipped his beer and the way he leaned his elbow on the table, she had a feeling that just the opposite was true. She had a feeling that the gorgeously tailored shirt he was wearing was simply the first shirt he'd seen in his closet. And that the touch of gel in his hair that seemed to make him shine that much more had simply been thrown on as an afterthought when he got out of the shower. There seemed to be not the slightest bit of effort involved. He was, without an ounce of awareness, perfect.

She walked a few steps closer, heart now pulsing somewhere in her throat, and waited patiently for him to notice her. And when his face drifted up from his glass of beer. . . he noticed. He noticed in such a way as to leave her with no other choice but to fall in love with him permanently.

His eyes froze over with that certain Spielbergian childlike wonder, as if some heavenly white alien light had just shone in his eyes for the first time. "Oh my God," he uttered. "Oh, my sweet, sweet Lord."

Yes. Thank you. Thank you all. I knew this was the right choice. I knew it. She matched his childlike wonderment with a shy smile of her own and took her seat.

"You look. . ." Josh gave up on words and just slowly shook his head.

"My party dress," she offered humbly, turning out her hands ever so slightly to officially present herself.

"Yes," he declared with a nod. "Yes. That *is* your party dress. That is just. . ." He returned to the shaking of his head. "I'm just. . . I'm so glad we didn't go to Starbucks."

Heather laughed a too loud laugh, quickly realizing just how overwhelmingly nervous she was. Every time his eyes swept over her, it was like he was pressing some kind of adrenaline button on the back of her neck that made her whole body just want to spin and spin until she'd worked out all the excess energy.

It was another minute or so before she even realized there was a pink drink sitting right in front of her. "What's this?" she asked excitedly.

"I ordered you a drink," he said, still staring at her with hypnotic awe. "I hope you don't mind."

"What is it?" She smiled.

"It's the specialty of the house," he said. "The Pink Poodle."

"Well that was very *sweet*," she cooed. "But I should warn you. After about two sips of alcohol. . . I can't be held accountable for my actions. You'll have to take care of me, okay?"

Josh locked his overpowering blue gaze on her, sending a flush of heat through her face. "I would be *honored* to take care of you," he said, bringing Heather's pounding heart flying up to somewhere around her chin. "But if you don't want this drink, that's totally—"

"No, I trust you." She giggled, grabbing the cocktail off the table quickly. She hadn't meant to appear quite so desperate, but she was absolutely dying for something to calm the volcanic jitters in her stomach. She took a careful sip of the drink and found it to be quite possibly the most delicious thing she had ever tasted—she couldn't even taste the slightest hint of alcohol. "Mmm," she said with a smile. "Excellent choice."

"Why, *thank you*," he replied with the inflection of the world's most debonair gentleman.

The humor of his response trickled off, suddenly leaving the two of them in a long, silent eye lock that doubled the jitters in Heather's stomach. She quickly took two more large gulps of the sugary drink, realizing she'd practically finished it already.

"Uh-oh," Josh said, flashing her his breathtaking grin. "I think you just passed your two-sip limit."

"I know," she squeaked with embarrassment, looking down at the nearly empty glass.

"Well. . . ?" he inquired with a chuckle. "Are you drunk yet?"

Heather paused to check her body for an honest answer. "*Plastered,*" she said with a laugh, dropping her face in her hands as Josh began to giggle. "I *told* you, it's ridiculous!" She looked up and darted her eyes quickly to her left and right, leaning her face in much closer to his with a naughty smile. "Can I have another?"

THE PHONE'S SHRILL RING WOKE

Gaia from another deeply unsatisfying semisleep—the only kind she'd been capable of outside of Ed's bed. She rolled her fully clothed body over the bit of sheet still on the bed and squinted at the time.

1 A.M. Who the hell is calling me at 1 A.M.? Oh God, Ed, please don't do this. Don't start calling me at all hours of the morning, or I swear to God, I'll crack.

The ring was never ending and more irritating by the second. Whoever it was, they had no intention of giving up. Tatiana raised her perfectly coifed head off her pillow and complained from across the room. "Who is this?" she croaked angrily, obviously awoken from a perfect sleep that matched her perfect hair and her perfect little silk jammies.

"How the hell should I know?" Gaia snapped. "What am I, psychic?"

"It is probably your foul-mouthed friend calling to tell you who she has robbed this evening."

"Why don't you shut your ignorant mouth," Gaia whispered as she leaped out of bed and stumbled to the phone. Maybe it *was* Gen. "At least Gen's honest about who she is."

"What is that supposed to mean?"

"Gee, I don't know. But you better get some sleep if you want to be ready for morning coffee with Ed."

"I don't know what you're talking about," Tatiana hissed, throwing her pillow over her head to block out the incessant ringing.

Gaia grabbed the phone off the receiver, snapping it to her ear. "Hello?"

"Gaia?" the voice whimpered under the loud din of

traffic noises. It was Gen's voice, breaking up in the horrible static of a city pay phone.

Gen was whimpering? Bad sign. Very bad sign.

"What's wrong?" Gaia demanded, barking loudly into the phone.

"Shhh!" Tatiana huffed from under her pillow.

Gaia slapped her hand over the phone. "Shut your freakin' mouth," she growled, throwing the phone back to her ear. "Gen, are you still there? I looked all over for you today. What the hell happened?"

"I *know*," Gen replied. "I feel like such shit for leaving you in there alone. I'm *so sorry*. I had to run. I thought you were going to follow me."

"Don't worry about it; it's fine. Listen, I don't think you're going to have to worry anymore because—"

"I *am* worried," Gen interrupted urgently. There was a kind of fear in her voice that Gaia didn't even think Gen was capable of. "Gaia, I think he's following me."

"Who? *Casper?*"

"*Yes.* I think he's been tailing me all day, and I've got to tell you, Gaia, after the shit that went down today, I'm freaked. I really am."

Gaia couldn't believe it. She just couldn't fathom how Casper would possibly mess with Gen after the very clear warning Gaia had given him. Could she have underestimated him that badly? Or had she just totally lost her touch?

"Gaia, are you there?"

"I'm here," she said, picturing Casper's pathetic face and what she was going to do to it this time. What she should have just done in the first place. That was when her anger gave way to the reality of the situation. The only reason Casper was on Gen's trail. . . was that Gaia had let him go. She nearly began hammering the phone against Tatiana's perfectly organized desk.

Stupid, stupid, stupid. When the hell are you going to learn? Kill them first. Warn them later.

She was *still* reliving her mistakes with Mary. Still.

"Where can I meet you?" Gaia asked urgently. "Tell me where, and I'll be there in five minutes. *Less* than five minutes. I'm going to fix this, Gen, I swear. I'm going to solve this problem. He is *not* going to hurt you."

"I just don't know. . . ," Gen moaned. "I don't know if anyplace out here is safe. Is anyone home at your house?"

Gaia looked over at Tatiana's angry eyes peeking around her pillow. She couldn't care less what Tatiana thought. But Natasha could be a problem. "Just hold on, okay?"

She dropped the phone on the desk and sprinted to Natasha's bedroom, pulling on the reins before carefully creaking open the door. . . .

Gone again. As per usual, Natasha had gone out for one of her mysterious late night excursions. Gaia didn't want to know what kind of crap her freaky fake mom was up to every night—strip

184

clubs? Late night bingo? She didn't even care. She was just thankful for any additional hours that she wasn't home. Particularly right now. Gaia sprinted back to the phone.

"Are you still there?"

"I'm here," Gen said, "but I'm going to run out of quarters, Gaia. What the hell am I going to do?"

"The coast is clear here," Gaia said. "It's totally cool. Just get your ass over here. Get your ass over here now and I will deal with this, okay? I swear to God."

"You're sure no one else is home?"

"I'm sure," Gaia said. "Just Princess Prissy Bitch, that's it. You'll be safe here."

"Okay," Gen said. "Okay, I'll be there."

The line went dead. Gaia slammed the phone down on the floor and began planning Casper's murder.

I know I should feel guilty
tonight. Natasha and I have
crossed an imaginary line that no
amount of my intense repression
or denial can erase.

But in spite of a slew of moral
doubts, I know I'm not a liar.
And the honest truth is. . . I
don't feel guilty. I simply feel
alive again.

I'd really done nothing but
dig a larger and larger hole for
myself, inch by inch. And Natasha
has simply swooped in and lifted
me out of that hole with such
amazing ease. Just a gentle
touch, kind brown eyes, some
well-placed optimism, and a kiss.
That was really all it took to
resuscitate a heart that had just
about given over to self-pity.

The truth is, everything has
become so much easier now.
Tonight I could look into her
eyes without punishing myself.
Tonight I could let my eyes coast
freely over the tiny creases in
the corners of her mouth when she

TOM

smiled and the gentle curves of
her lips when she spoke. Tonight
I couldn't help but marvel at
life's totally nonsensical,
totally unscientific nature. It
just amazes me that a man could
go from being so alone—so
unequivocally, permanently alone—
to being so. . . *not* alone, in
one night. Not even one night,
but one hour, one minute.

One kiss.

"WELL, TONIGHT THE REPORT IS
delightfully simple," Natasha said, holding both of Tom's hands firmly. They were seated in the corner of the same Clinton Street bar as the night before, though things were now obviously very different. "Gaia is at home. And she is *asleep*. A miracle, no?" Natasha smiled, and Tom let himself study every aspect of her face that he'd missed in the last few days of avoiding eye contact.

Foul White Wine

How very like Tom's brilliant daughter to pick this night not to embroil herself in any further mortal danger. It was as if even she, who probably hated Tom as much as she ever had right now, knew that Tom deserved at least one night of sweetness and light. And affection.

Not until today had Tom really begun to understand what effect deprivation could have on one's psyche. The way he had begun to obsess over his brother at the expense of everything else—at the expense of the simplest of pleasures or even the occasional genuine smile. He'd really done nothing but dig a larger and larger hole for himself. And Natasha had lifted him out of that hole with such amazing ease.

"Yes," Tom agreed, giving in to his shamefully adolescent lover's gaze. "A miracle. I couldn't agree more."

"My God." She laughed, letting her head fall forward.

"What?" Tom asked, watching her long strands of hair cascade onto the cracked old wooden table.

"I don't know," she said with a smile, tossing back her hair as she raised her eyes to the ceiling. "I am having the flashbacks to early motherhood. The baby. . . she is *finally* asleep for a change, uh? We have finally put Gaia to bed at. . ." She looked at her watch. "One in the morning. So we have earned one drink, no?"

"Absolutely," Tom agreed, clinking glasses with her as they sipped their foul white wine happily.

Tom was in awe at how seriously Natasha took her duties as Gaia's guardian—as if she were Gaia's own mother. There was no question about it. He had chosen wisely. He could not possibly have picked a better guardian for his daughter.

"*Eh-hem,*" a voice chimed in from behind him.

Nothing annoyed Tom more than the passive-aggressive clearing of the throat to gain attention. But he didn't stay annoyed when he turned and saw George Niven behind him.

"George!" Tom celebrated, rising out of his chair and giving him a hard slap on the back. "What are you doing here?"

Tom hoped that George might have come as a peaceful gesture after the unfortunate argument they'd had in their last meeting. But he could already tell from the look on George's face that wasn't going to happen.

George gave Natasha a barely polite half nod and

quarter smile and then turned to Tom. "They told me I could find you here." He gave Natasha a quick once-over, then stared into Tom's eyes. "Can we speak privately for a moment?"

Tom felt all his hard-earned sweetness and light deflating from his chest as Natasha's beautiful smile slowly disappeared. She turned away and focused on her drink.

"George," Tom said, sighing, "anything you need to say to me, you can say in front of Natasha."

George glanced at Natasha one last time and then gripped Tom's arm. "Tom, please. I'm very sorry to, uh, *interrupt*, but I promise you this will take only a minute. I'm sorry," he muttered to Natasha, barely turning in her direction.

Tom let out another, much larger sigh. "Fine," he agreed. He leaned across the table toward Natasha. "I promise I'll just be a minute," he said, apologizing profusely with his eyes.

"Of course," Natasha said, presenting a wide fake smile to both Tom and George.

"Thanks," he said, smiling back and flashing her a look that was meant to remind her of their new and much deeper connection. Natasha squeezed his hand and gazed back at him, letting him know with her eyes that the connection would still be alive and well when he returned to the table. Tom then walked resentfully to other side of the bar as George followed.

"Okay, what was that all about?" Tom asked, glaring at George.

"I'm sorry, Tom. I'm just concerned about *her*," he said, throwing a quick but pointed glance in Natasha's direction. "I've been asking around, trying to find out exactly how much the other agents know about her, and the answer, Tom, is always 'very little.'"

"George, we've been through this." Tom cast his eyes past George's shoulder to make sure Natasha was all right. "Now, the last thing I want is for us to fight anymore, *please*. You need to get to know her. You need to understand what a valuable member of our team she's become. I'd trust her with my life, George."

"That's exactly what I'm afraid of, Tom," he whispered intensely. "You're trusting her with Gaia's life as well, but I ask you again, how much do you actually *know* about Galina?"

"George, please, you're being ridiculous," Tom replied, wishing the situation didn't call for such a low volume. "Aren't we all a little too familiar for code names? You can call her *Natasha*."

"Well, I would prefer to keep this particular relationship on a professional level, Tom. So, if you don't mind, the rest of the Agency and I will continue to refer to her by her *professional* name. And if you don't mind my asking, just how *familiar* is your relationship? Because when I walked in, it looked *extremely* familiar—"

"All right, that's *enough*," Tom said in a strained voice,

realizing he'd been loud enough for one of the patron's heads to turn. "That's enough," he said more quietly.

The two of them took a moment to calm themselves. George dropped his head and then raised it again slowly to meet Tom's eyes. "Look, I'm sorry," he said in a much kinder tone. "I don't want us to fight again any more than you do. If anything, I wanted to apologize for being so stubborn last time. I'm just trying to help you. Tom, she's not to be trusted."

"George, *don't*—"

"But that's not why I came to see you," George interrupted, raising his hand quickly to make peace. "We were able to obtain a little more information. It's not much, but it's a start, and I wanted to get it to you as soon as possible."

Tom felt a bolt of energy that instantly straightened his posture. He'd been waiting on a lead for days, anything at all. "Go on," he said, feeling his heart pick up speed.

George reached into his jacket pocket and handed Tom a small white envelope. "Anything we've gotten so far is in there. There are a fair amount of indications that Loki. . . we're not too *familiar* with him to call him 'Loki,' I hope?"

Tom rolled his eyes.

"Sorry," George muttered. "Anyway, we've gotten word that he may be setting up some kind of HQ in the Cayman Islands. We've intercepted a few real estate inquiries through one of his dummy companies, and we may be able to trace a couple of questionable shell accounts that were just opened at the national bank."

"Then I know where I'm going," Tom said, shoving the envelope in his coat pocket.

"Yes," George said. "We figured you'd say that. They've already fueled up the plane."

"Good," Tom said. He placed his hands on George's shoulders and looked him in the eye. "This is good, George. Thank you."

George gave him a firm hug. "Just promise me you'll keep your eyes open, Tom. That's all I'm asking. Keep them open."

"Of course," Tom assured him. "Of course."

Tom peered back over George's shoulder and met Natasha's eyes. She flashed him a stunning, wide-open smile, and Tom suddenly felt horribly guilty. How could he have left such a magnificent creature alone at a table for so long?

WHEN GAIA OPENED HER DOOR,

Gen's face looked whiter than usual. Seeing Gen looking even remotely afraid stung Gaia's chest and made her unbearably uncomfortable. It was all Gaia's fault. She'd showered Casper with all those threats and then just left Gen alone with him in the park to bear the aftermath. *Sloppy, Gaia. So short-sighted and sloppy.*

She pulled Gen into the apartment and slammed the door shut, locking both locks and dragging Gen through the living room. "You're going to be fine now. Don't even sweat that asshole. I'm going to deal with him."

"I don't know, Gaia," she said, speaking in that same near whimper Gaia had heard over the phone. She collapsed on the couch and pulled her cigarettes out of her pocket. "If you'd seen his face, you'd be freaking out, too."

"You can't smoke in here," Gaia said. Cigarette smoke made her thoroughly ill.

Gen froze with her lighter nearly to her cigarette and gave Gaia the remotest glimpse of a pissed-off look. But her expression snapped back to distraught almost instantly. "I'm just kind of freaking out here," she explained. "Maybe a half of one . . . ?"

"I'll get us some doughnuts."

Gaia ran to the kitchen and grabbed a box of doughnuts and two sodas from the fridge. She ran back to the living room, handed Gen her soda, dropped the doughnuts on the coffee table, and collapsed on the couch next to her. "So what happened?"

Gen was incredibly fidgety. Tapping her feet, scratching at her face, flipping her hair back a thousand times. It was pretty scary how nervous a smoker could get without a cigarette. "He was just. . . everywhere I turned, you know? In the park, whenever I ate. . . . I tried to hop a few subways around town, and he was *still there*, looking like he wanted to cut my goddamn throat, you know? I mean, I don't get scared of much, but his look was *scary*, Gaia. Seriously scary. I mean, if I go back out there tonight. . . I don't know. I just don't know. . . ."

"Well, maybe I should go out there and look for him," Gaia said. "I bet he followed you here, too." She got up from the couch, but Gen grabbed her arm, flashing her that same disturbing look of worry.

"No, don't go, okay?" Gen asked quietly, averting her eyes. She was obviously embarrassed to be looking and sounding so needy. Gaia tried to skip over it as quickly as possible.

"Okay, but we should do *something*, you know?" Gaia insisted. "Trust me, I know how this stuff works. If we don't send a serious message to him right now, then you're never going to be safe out there. He's just waiting for his moment now." Gaia hated rubbing it in—how totally right all her warnings to Gen had been—but this was as vulnerable as she'd probably seen Gen in the brief time she'd known her, and now was the time to hammer her point home. "You're going to find yourself alone at the wrong time, in the wrong place," she stated. "And then you're dead."

"I know," Gen agreed, looking even more nervous. "That's why I thought. . . No, forget it. Forget it."

"What?" Gaia asked. "You thought what?"

Gen dropped her head down slightly and watched herself fiddle with her fingers. "Well, I thought, maybe. . . since he's out *there*, you know. . . maybe I'd be cool in here."

"You are," Gaia agreed. "You're fine here."

"No, I mean. . . I thought maybe I could *stay* here, you know, tonight. It would be just for one night," she added quickly. "I mean, I could totally figure something else out after that."

Gaia had two very quick thoughts. One: She couldn't believe Gen would let herself be that needy right to Gaia's face. She was obviously very seriously scared. Two: If Gen stayed in that house, then Natasha would go completely insane when she got home. She would become irrevocably freaked out.

That was a good enough reason right there.

But Gaia wouldn't have said no, anyway. Protecting Gen from Casper had become much too big a priority for her. In fact, it was one of the few priorities she had left, besides avoiding all humankind.

"Don't be a freak—of course you can stay here," Gaia said, looking Gen in the eye. "You just can't do drugs if you're going to be in my house."

"I thought it wasn't your house," Gen pointed out annoyingly.

"Whatever." Gaia sighed. "No drugs, okay?"

"*Okay*, no drugs," Gen said. "Well. . . *thanks*." She

jumped out of the couch with a huge, long sigh of relief.

"No problem." Gaia smiled.

"So. . ." Gen looked around the apartment slowly. "Where do I sleep? 'Cause I don't know about you, but I am freakin' *burnt* from this day."

"Yeah," Gaia agreed. "Me too. Let's hope tomorrow's not quite so unfortunate. Come on." She grabbed Gen's arm and pulled her into the bedroom.

"Oh, shit," Gen laughed the second she stepped into the bedroom. "What the hell is this? You live in the girlie bedroom from hell."

"I *know*. Shut your mouth."

"Yes, I agree," Tatiana yelled from her bed. "Shut your mouth!"

Gen looked over at the bed and threw her hand over her mouth. "Oh, no way," she moaned, looking back at Gaia with heartfelt pity. "You share a freakin' *room* with Princess Prissy Bitch? You live in the girlie room from hell. . . with the *girlie girl* from hell? *Bah-hahaha*. . ."

Gen dropped to the floor, laughing hysterically at Gaia's misfortune. Her mood had certainly improved since Gaia told her she could stay.

Tatiana sat up in her bed and gave Gen a look of purely murderous intent. "What is she doing in this house?"

"She's going to be staying the night," Gaia said.

"What are you talking about?"

"You heard her." Gen laughed. "I'm staying the

night." Gen affected the look of a concerned mother. "Oh, don't be scared, Princess Prissy Bitch. Gaia will protect you from me."

"Yeah, right," Gaia muttered. "That'll happen."

Tatiana looked up to Gaia with a piercing stare. "Gaia. . . please tell me this is not serious."

"Go back to bed," Gaia said. "Just go to sleep."

"Gaia, you make a terrible mistake if—"

"A mistake?" Gen shouted. "A *mistake?*" She made a move toward Tatiana, but Gaia held her back. "*You're* the only mistake around here, *bitch.*" She turned back to Gaia in a huff. "Gaia, we don't really have to sleep in here with Princess Prissy Bitch, right? Tell me there's somewhere else we can sleep. Someplace *private.*"

Gaia gave Tatiana one last hateful glance. "The den," she said. "Let's sleep in the den."

"The den," Gen agreed. "Definitely the den." She gave Tatiana a menacing stare as she backed out of the room. "Who knows?" she whispered tauntingly. "Hopefully when we come back to this room. . . Princess Prissy Bitch will have magically disappeared."

Memo

From: G
To: L

    Connection has been secured. Invitation exchanged. Expect company within three hours.

Memo

From: L
To: G

    Three-hour ETA understood and confirmed. Proceed to level-two2 infiltration and report on results.

Each moment of
the last ten
minutes had
only served to
inform her   **fetal**
of what an
absolute   **ball**
imbecile she
was when it
came to
people.

Ungiggly Gaze

"WHOA, SLOW IT DOWN THERE, buddy." Heather giggled uncontrollably. She gripped Josh's arm as though she were hanging on for dear life. "I told you to take it slow."

Heels and drinking, Heather. Heels and drinking. Mental note: Next time you drink. . . sneakers. Big ones. Big flat ones.

Josh stopped in the middle of East Fourth Street and placed his arm around her waist to help hold her up. "I'm sorry," he said, laughing. "I didn't realize just how slow was slow."

"*Sloooow.*" She pulled on the lapels of his coat and gazed up at his eyes. "I like to take it *real slooooow.*" She tucked her head into his chest, collapsing into another long laughing fit. "You know. . . ," she squeaked, as if she were just about to make an earth-shattering scientific discovery. "I think. . . I'm drunk." Then she gave in to the giggles again.

"Yeah, I think you might be right about that one." Josh grinned. "I think I might be, too."

"Mm-hmm." Heather nodded. "Yeah. That sounds about right. What the hell was in those Pink Poodles? And more important. . . how many did I have?" More giggles.

"Well. . ." Josh considered. "I don't know, and. . . I don't know."

"Mm-hmm, yeah, well. . . I am *pretty damn sure*. . . that I'm drunk."

"Yes, indeed," Josh agreed, swaying slightly from side to side with Heather as they tried to make it down the next block. "We need to keep walking. The fresh air. . . That's going to solve our little problem."

"Yes," Heather agreed. "Walking. Yes. But you just remember, Josh Brown." She stopped him in the street and grabbed his lapels again. "I am now drunk. And you have to take care of me."

"Always." He smiled.

The way he said *always* left Heather melting, swooning, and most likely a few inches off the ground—if she'd been able to feel her feet, she could have been sure. "*Really?*" she mused, playing the romantic lead in some old sappy movie. "*Always?* You promise?"

"I promise," Josh nodded.

The way he'd answered was far more serious than Heather's jokey question, and it left them locked in a most ungiggly gaze for what felt like half an hour. Heather gripped his lapels, and Josh's arms held her waist to keep her from falling. She pored over his face from this delectably close distance. He was more beautiful the closer she got.

"You know what?" he murmured.

"What?" she whispered.

Josh suddenly lifted Heather's entire body. She let out a series of giggly hoots and squeals, not having expected

202

this at all. He swung her around to the building on their left and pressed his body closer to hers, leaning her up against the wall. Heather's heartbeat quadrupled.

Josh lowered his head and let his face graze hers fom all sides as she continued to hold tight to his lapels. "Is this okay?" he whispered.

"Yes," she uttered, barely able to breathe as his hands slid under her coat. Each hand felt twice the size of her waist as he ran his fingers along her skintight dress. She let out the slightest gasp as he surprised her again, suddenly pulling her waist closer to his, even though their bodies couldn't really have gotten any closer.

She let go of his lapels and lifted her arms higher, wrapping them around his neck and clasping her fingers as she pulled his head closer. She could really no longer accept having his lips anywhere else other than against her own.

He leaned down and kissed her deeply, letting the passion of his kiss press her body more firmly up against the wall. God, this was every bit as good as she had dreamed it would be.

"Listen," he whispered, kissing her ear between words. "We should go somewhere. Do you want to go somewhere?"

"Uh-huh," she said. "Yes. Anywhere. Where?"

He cupped her face in his hand and kissed her again, leaving them almost no time to breathe—not that Heather could breathe anymore with him touching her like this. "My dorm is too far," he said.

"My house is out," she whispered, leaving out all of the details.

"Ugh," Josh grunted with short-breathed frustration, dropping his head against her shoulder. "There's *got* to be somewhere close," he said. "Because I'm going *crazy* here."

"Me too," Heather breathed. "*Close.* Close is good."

Josh pulled his head away for a second and looked in either direction down Fourth Street. "I've *got* it," he said.

"Where?"

"The park," he said. "Washington Square Park—it's right up there."

Heather suddenly felt the slightest bit of nausea mix in with all the thrills that were coursing through her body. The park? Ugh. She knew it was close, and *God, yes,* did she want someplace close, but that park? Did it have to be *that* park? She hadn't been in there at night since her attack. Of course she hadn't. How could she possibly go in there at night?

"I don't know. . . ." She wavered.

"No?" he asked, leaning in and kissing her again. "You're sure? It's perfect."

His kisses were every bit as good as all his other unbelievably perfect qualities, and thinking about anything other than his body was next to impossible, but still... "I know it is, but..."

"Oh God, your attack," he remembered, pulling back. Heather nodded.

"You've never been back there since?"

"Not at night," she said.

"Well, *let's go*," he said with his confident smile, grabbing her hands. "Heather, that there is one of the most beautiful parks in New York City and some group of assholes have ruined it for you. Let's go in there right now and *un* ruin it. Let's go in there and do something *unforgettable*." The way he said *unforgettable* sent a shock of warm sparks down her spine. "Then you'll have a perfect new memory to replace the old horrible one," he said. He leaned in and kissed her firmly on the lips. "Come on, we'll do it together. Let's reclaim that park and make it *ours*. Besides, I told you. . . I'm taking care of you tonight. Nothing bad is going to happen to you as long as I'm around, Heather. Nothing."

She absolutely adored his total assurance. His total enthusiasm. It was so childlike and completely. . . fearless. That's what she loved about Josh. He just wanted what he wanted, and he followed all his impulses. It was so inspiring when he was around. Everything seemed so much simpler, so much less daunting and intimidating—so much more possible. It made Heather feel stronger. It made her want to do and say what *she* wanted, too.

If Josh could be fearless, then so could she.

She placed his face in her hands and devoured his lips with her own, giving him the longest, most passionate kiss she was capable of giving. Then she tugged on his hand and led him toward Washington Square Park. "Let's go," she said, smiling.

"You're sure?" he called out as she began running for the park.

"Hurry up!" she shouted back as she pulled off her impossible shoes. She could run a few blocks in stockings. Sure, she could. Tonight she could do whatever she wanted to do.

"ED?"

Somewhere between sleep and waking, Gaia had convinced herself that she was back in bed with him. Back safely tucked  away under his rumpled purple sheets, his arm wrapped around her waist and his breath ruffling her hair gently in the rhythm of sound sleep. Back when quiet had been a good thing and not just blank space to be filled up with all her loud, self-pitying thoughts.

But of course, there were no arms around her. None of those soothing sounds of the street passing through his window. No shafts of light that cast blue shadows on his ceiling. Nothing but dull airy silence and pitch blackness.

Until she heard the clink. It was almost inaudible. It probably wouldn't have even been heard by the average ear, but Gaia picked it up immediately. In fact, it was probably what had woken her up in the first place. A clink here and a clink there, barely even tapping her eardrums.

She got up off the carpet and moved to turn on a light. Unfortunately, she had never even been to the den in the daytime, let alone slept there at night, so finding a lamp was something of an adventure. After a minute or so of flailing her arms, she finally bumped into something lamp shade–like. She reached under and switched it on.

Not only was there no Ed in sight. But there was no Gen, either.

Clink.

There it was again. Coming from the living room. And there was the slightest paranoid buzz, nagging her like a cold that wouldn't quite die. Why were there quiet clinks in the living room, and where the hell was Gen?

Jesus, Gaia, relax. She probably just went to get a drink of water. Maybe Natasha finally came home.

She decided to take her approach to the living room very slowly. If it was nothing, then she could turn back before she got caught looking like a timid paranoid housewife. If it was something, then she'd be able to catch that something red-handed. There was only one possibility that truly worried her. Something she'd totally forgotten to check on before falling asleep next to her new friend in the den.

Drugs. Gen probably still had a stash of her own, and Gaia had foolishly neglected to confiscate it. *Think next time, Gaia.* She was so new at this drug-counseling thing, maybe she was entitled to a few mistakes. But still, if she found Gen doing drugs in the living room, she was going to feel like a totally inept friend.

She stepped to the door of the living room and poked her head around. There was hardly any light to see by, but enough was coming from the open windows to see that something in the room did not look right.

Things were missing.

The silver bowl was gone from the coffee table, and there were no little green lights where the VCR had been. A thief? Was that what she was dealing with here? A goddamn petty thief?

Wait a minute. Casper. It had to be Casper. Anything with the word *petty* attached to it had to be Casper. Of course. He'd been tailing Gen all day. He must have followed her straight to Gaia's house and just waited for all the lights in the apartment to go out before he moved in. But how did he break in? Maybe he was a better petty thief than she would have figured him for.

She stepped carefully through the doorway and searched the room, but it was still too dark to see enough. She tiptoed to the lamp by the couch and reached to turn it on.

But it went on all by itself.

"*Boo*," came the voice from behind her. Followed by a very self-satisfied giggle.

Unbelievable. Just absolutely unbelievable that he would want to mess with Gaia again. Was this asshole a glutton for punishment or what? She whipped around to face him. But instead she was facing the barrel of his gun pointed at the middle of her forehead. *Dammit. I knew I should have taken all three guns from the boathouse.*

"Guess who?" He grinned, holding tightly to a laundry bag full of Natasha's belongings. "Yeah." He chuckled repulsively. "Thought you were never going to see me again, right? Yeah, gee, I guess I messed up your little agreement, huh? You *bitch*." The smile turned into something psychotic and vicious as he cracked the gun over the side of Gaia's head. The impact was excruciating, but Gaia quickly bounced her head back up and gave him her most defiant stare. She was not going to show him an ounce of pain. *Her* pain, that is. She'd show him plenty of his own.

"How the hell did you get in here?" she demanded.

"How?" he asked. "I *told* you, I'm the friendly ghost. I can walk through walls."

"Where's Gen?" she asked, loosening her fingers in preparation to snap his neck once she got her answer.

"Oh, why?" he teased. "Are you worried about your little charity case? Isn't that sweet."

Gaia could feel nothing but sadistic and violent tendencies at this point. The thoughts of what he might have done to Gen were bringing out the kind of rage he really didn't want to face. She had begun to think of the specific ways she would have to torture him before she killed him. Sick scenarios that simply were not repeatable. "You tell me where she is right now or—"

"Or what?" Casper challenged, shoving the barrel of his gun directly into the skin between her eyes. "Or you'll get shot in the head? Yeah, I think you may be right about that."

"Tell me what the hell you did to her!" she howled, gearing up her limbs for a full-scale attack.

But before she could make a move, an arm crept over her shoulder and held a knife flat up against her neck. *More thugs? How many dudes work for this loser?*

"Boo!" a girl's voice whispered in her ear. *A girl's voice?*

Casper dropped his gun and started to laugh in Gaia's face. Just stood there, laughing, with his hand over his mouth. And then the girl with the knife to Gaia's throat began laughing as well—straight into Gaia's ear. Gaia already knew who was laughing; she just didn't want to believe it. She didn't want to believe this was happening. But she at least needed to confirm it. She leaned her head back slightly to try and get a glimpse of her. And get a glimpse she did.

Yep. That's what she had thought. *You idiot, Gaia.*
You unadulterated idiot.

She'd finally found Gen. Not another thug with a
knife to Gaia's throat. *Gen* with a knife to Gaia's throat.

"Hey, *buddy*," Gen whispered in her ear. Casper
was nearly falling down laughing at this point.

"Gen, what are you doing?" Gaia asked. As if she
didn't already know. She kept her head as still as possible
since Gen had the knife nearly slicing into her throat.

"What am I doing?" Gen asked. "I'm *robbing* your
ass, you idiot. What does it look like I'm doing?" She
turned to Casper. "I told you she wasn't that smart,"
she said with a laugh.

Yeah. That's what she thought she was doing. Gaia
closed her eyes in the darkest kind of humiliation. The reality of the situation was very slowly
beginning to seep from her pores, through her brain,
and finally, most painfully, into her heart, where she'd
found it the hardest to accept this despicable truth.

She'd made a mistake. She'd made a terrible, terrible, idiotic, stupid mistake.

"Oh, what's the matter?" Gen asked with mock concern. "Did someone ruin your little do-gooder project
for the week? You poor little thing. Now you won't
have your drug-addict charity case for show-and-tell
tomorrow."

Gaia didn't even bother responding. There was no
point in adding to her humiliation.

"Yeah," Gen went on, "here's your news flash, Kung Fu Barbie: I'm not your poor little dead rich girlfriend, and I don't need *saving*. What I need is all the Princess Prissy Bitch accessories in this apartment. *That's* what I need. So thanks for *finally* inviting me in. It took you long enough."

Gaia felt abundantly sick to her stomach.

How could she have been so hopelessly gullible? She was trained to detect lies just from the shifting of the eyes or the staggering of breaths in a sentence. She was trained in every aspect of profiling, trained to detect what character elements naturally combined to make an untrustworthy person or a potential criminal. Yet here she was. . . totally suckered by a lying junkie and some two-bit dealer who looked like an ugly Backstreet Boy. *That's* how lonely Gaia had become. That's how desperate for some purpose in life. That's how much she loved and missed Mary Moss.

And Gen was sure as hell right about one thing. She was no Mary. That strip of fake red hair should have been the tip-off. She was a fake. A total fake.

"And you know what?" Gen went on. "I am so glad our little scam here is done, Gaia, because I am so *sick* of listening to your condescending crap. I don't even know where you get off, thinking *you're* going to fix *my* life? Your life's the most screwed-up pathetic shit I've ever seen."

She was right about that, too.

"Suggestion," Gen added. "Instead of trying to turn me into some chick who's already dead. . . why don't you find yourself *one* real freakin' friend? 'Cause your shit is tragic. It's so tragic, I almost feel guilty scamming you. Except I don't."

"Yeah, that's real sweet," Casper said. "You done with your little speech? Because it is freakin' *payback* time. Where's the other one?"

"In there," Gen said, motioning to the bedroom with her head. "Now, this. . . ," she whispered in Gaia's ear, "this, I think you're going to like."

"YOU DIDN'T TELL ME SHE WAS SO

Reverse Snobbery

hot," Casper announced as he pushed Tatiana through the bedroom doorway, holding his gun to the back of her head.

Tatiana gazed coldly into Gaia's eyes as Casper shoved her toward a chair at the dining table. Gaia winced when she saw her face. She didn't look terrified. She didn't look angry. Not quite stunned, even. She looked almost *resigned* to this horrific fate. It was as if Tatiana had already known something like this was going to happen the moment Gaia had brought Gen into their house. As if it had only been a matter of time before Gaia found some way to make an absolute mess of things—to get them robbed of all their precious family heirlooms and then to get them all killed. Tatiana had probably been expecting something like this from the moment she'd first seen Gaia in her bedroom, lying in a pool of sweat, hallucinating all kinds of paranoid murderous scenarios.

Gaia had despised Tatiana for every one of her offensive assumptions and lofty judgments. And they had all been correct. All Tatiana's holier-than-thou, high-and-mighty presumptions had been disgustingly, embarrassingly right on the money. Bringing this low-level hustler into the house had been a terrible mistake. *Terrible mistake*—there was the understatement of the century. Gaia's lousy judgment and reverse snobbery were about to get them both killed.

No, it wasn't even that. It wasn't just the reverse snobbery or the lousy judgment. It was the curse. The Curse of Gaia Moore. Apparently being in close proximity to Gaia was really the *only* necessary qualification to fall prey to the curse. Gaia didn't even have to like the person. Yes, she despised Tatiana. But she'd never wished something like this on her. Never.

"Oh, man," Casper complained. "I can't believe I'm going to blow holes in this beautiful head."

"Will you shut up with that?" Gen snapped, keeping

the knife secured to Gaia's throat. "She looks like she was made in a goddamn factory."

"Yeah, well. . . either way, she's gone."

Oh, Jesus. Find the way out of this, Gaia. What is the way out? She could think of nothing. Not one viable option. Gen and Casper probably didn't even know how cleverly they'd placed themselves, but nonetheless it was practically foolproof. They were simply too far apart for Gaia to do anything. If she made a move on Gen, there was no way she could get to Casper fast enough before he pulled the trigger.

"This is ridiculous," Gaia complained, trying to stall. "What does she have to do with any of this?"

"Oh, that's real simple," Casper said, running his gun through Tatiana's hair. "You messed up my friends bad, so I'm going to mess up yours. Eye for an eye and all that."

"She's not even my friend," Gaia said coldly, searching desperately for the remotest inkling of a plan.

Casper shrugged. "Yeah, well, Gen says you don't have any friends, so she's going to have to do."

"That doesn't make any sense," Gaia argued. "*I'm* the one who messed up your friends. You should kill me, not her."

"Who said we weren't going to do you?" Casper spat, looking more and more pissed off. "I think it's time you shut your mouth and watched. Now you can see what it feels like when someone pops a bullet right through one of your friends."

"I didn't even *shoot* your friends," Gaia hollered. "They shot each other."

"I told you to shut the hell up!" Casper growled, ripping Tatiana's head back by her hair and jabbing the gun into her left temple.

"Just shoot her already," Gen complained. "Gaia doesn't even like her. She hates the haughty bitch's guts. She doesn't give a shit whether she lives or dies."

"All right!" Casper hollered, securing the gun against her head.

Tatiana's face had gone totally blank as Casper tugged on her head like it wasn't even attached to a body. All she could do was stare coldly at Gaia. Stare at her and curse her with her eyes as Casper pulled back the hammer of his gun.

Once he'd flipped back the hammer, that nagging paranoid buzz that had been gnawing at Gaia's stomach exploded into a sense of doom that shook her insides to the point of nearly vomiting. Fearful yet again when she needed to take action—it was hardly even a surprise now. She had scraped every ounce of her brain for a way out of this, and she'd failed to find one. So she stood there like a useless fool and apologized to Tatiana with her eyes. In this final moment, it seemed she was really no better than Tatiana. Just as wispy and timid. Just as utterly helpless.

"Say good-bye," Casper uttered. He tightened his outstretched arm and squeezed down slowly on the trigger. When Tatiana suddenly opened her mouth and began to spew out a vicious stream of Russian words directly at Gaia.

The volume and urgency of her voice had erupted from so completely out of nowhere that Casper actually flinched and let go of the trigger as he watched her growl with rage into Gaia's face.

"Holy crap." He laughed nervously, looking over at Gen. "Bitch scared the living daylights out of me. What the hell language is she speaking?"

"Russian," Gen said. "I think she's a little pissed at my buddy Gaia here." She smiled. "Either that or she's saying her prayers or some shit."

Gen was right about one thing. She was definitely pissed. But she wasn't saying prayers at all. Far from it. Gaia listened to each harsh word being shot at her like gunfire:

Get that pathetic helpless look off your face and work with me. If you think I'm going to let this needle-brained drug-dealing son of a bitch be my executioner, then you're truly out of your mind. Now, you listen to me. I am going to count to three, and then I am going to elbow this pathetic lowlife where it hurts. You do what you have to do, and we will get ourselves out of this. On three. Do you understand me?

"Okay," Gaia replied calmly.

She was simply too amazed by Tatiana to offer a more detailed response.

"Is she finished?" Casper laughed.

Without further ado, Tatiana began a slow and steady countdown in Russian.

Three. . . two. . . one. . .

Without moving an inch from her seated position, Tatiana whipped her sharp, bony elbow directly into the center of Casper's crotch, forcing out a high-pitched howl of agony as he dropped his gun and collapsed to the floor in a rolled-up fetal ball.

Gaia seized her moment instantly, taking hold of the arm that Gen had around her neck with both hands and flipping her tragically skinny frame about five feet in front of her. Gen screamed out in pain as her entire skeleton cracked against the glossy hardwood floor of the living room. There was no way a hundred-pound junkie was going to be getting up from that fall anytime soon.

Gaia rolled forward and grabbed the gun off the floor as Tatiana dropped to her knees and swiped up the knife. She quickly knelt over Gen and held the knife to her nose. Not that Gen would have been able to move, anyway.

Casper had managed to make it back up to a crouching position, when Gaia hit him with a vicious kick combination. First a side kick straight to his gut and then a sweeping roundhouse kick to his jaw, rocking his entire body into the dining-room chairs before he slid down into a heap on the floor.

Gaia quickly turned to Tatiana, speaking urgently in Russian. "Are you all right?" she asked.

"I'm fine," she replied in Russian. "But I want them out of here. I want them out of here now."

"You read my mind," Gaia replied.

Like clockwork, Gaia and Tatiana grabbed the mumbling, moaning Casper and dragged him straight across the floor right into the building's hallway.

"Let *me* get the other one," Gaia requested. Tatiana stepped out of the way and left a clear path for Gaia. Gaia stomped back into the room and lifted Gen into her arms as though she were a bag of trash, carrying her bony frame out into the hallway and dumping her on top of Casper's semiconscious body.

She got down on one knee and tapped Gen's half-conscious face a few times to get her attention. "You just keep doing what you're doing, Gen. You keep using, and you stick with him. . . you'll be dead in no time."

Gaia and Tatiana stepped into their apartment, but Gaia turned back with an afterthought. "We're going to open this door again in five minutes. If you're not gone. . . that will be bad."

"That will be very bad," Tatiana agreed.

Tatiana slammed the door closed.

After a few moments of recovery, Gaia and Tatiana walked slowly over to Casper's overstuffed Christmas bag and began to put the items back in their places.

"I don't think we need to tell my mother about this

night," Tatiana said as she examined the wiring on the back of the VCR.

Gaia froze for a moment as she was setting the silver bowl back on the coffee table. Each moment of the last ten minutes had only served to inform her of what an absolute imbecile she was when it came to people. "Thank you," she said quietly.

"*Da*," Tatiana replied even more quietly.

They worked in silence for another few moments until Gaia just had to ask something. "*'Hit him where it hurts?'*" she asked in Russian. "I didn't know they used that expression in Russia."

"This is not right?" Tatiana asked. "Where it hurts? This is not where I hit him?"

"No, it's perfect," Gaia said. "It's perfect. . . . That's exactly where you hit him."

"Good. That was where I wanted to hit him."

From: shred@alloymail.com
To: gaia13@alloymail.com
Time: 2:06 A.M.
Re: I will delete this

Gaia,

God, I wish I could understand what happened
that morning. I really, really do. I'm staring
over at my bed, or our bed, or whatever, and that
night that was only a few days ago. . . seems
like it was about ten years ago.

The thing is, I love you so much, Gaia, and I
could have sworn you loved me, too, and now it
seems like everything just fell out the window for
no apparent reason at all. And I mean EVERYTHING,
including the most important friendship in my life.

Can you explain ANY of this to me any better
than you have? Am I crazy, or did I see the
actual you for two seconds in the cafeteria this
afternoon? Wasn't that you? Can we just sit down
for a couple of normal minutes and talk it over?
The actual me and the actual you?

Yeah, I know, I know. Blahblahblahblahblah who
cares who cares, right??

<DELETE>

her identity
had fallen so
far into the
crapper that
she **purified**
could
no longer **hatred**
recognize
anyone else's
identity,
either.

Electro-magnet

WHAT ARE YOU DOING ON THIS train, Gaia? Do you know what you're doing on this train?

She knew; she just didn't want to tell herself. She was on the six train, heading down toward Ed's... *neighborhood.* Not heading down toward Ed's per se, just down toward his neighborhood. Because God knew she needed a break from the Upper East Side. A nice long break.

It was just something about this night. This night had sent her one very basic message above all others. That message:

This whole "new life" of yours. . . total, unmitigated disaster.

Indeed, every single choice Gaia had made in her "new life" had not just backfired. It had back-*exploded.* Sticking to the Upper East Side had only brought her to Central Park. Central Park had only introduced her to Gen and Casper. Befriending Gen had nearly gotten her and Tatiana robbed and killed. Bad choices. Nothing but bad choices.

And then there was the matter of her complete and utter misjudgment of both Tatiana and Gen. How could such a well-educated, perceptive person have gotten it so completely wrong? The only conclusion she could draw for herself was that her identity had fallen so far into the crapper that she could no longer recognize anyone else's identity, either. That was why she'd roamed out of that Seventy-second Street apartment and onto a train downtown at two in the morning. Because downtown at least had a few remnants of a Gaia she could recognize. A few tattered remains of something resembling "home." West Fourth Street. Washington Square Park.

And Ed. Of course Ed. Ed was home.

Her new life had in fact made her so ill that she'd actually found herself harking back to the days of the Perry Street town house and George and Ella Niven. Even that godforsaken place struck her as home tonight in her sickeningly glorified memories. And if those horrible days could feel like home. . . well, then things had gotten awfully bad.

She climbed out of the train at Astor Place and stood on the small, windy island, trying to pick a direction. Gray's Papaya would be closed. So would the Krispy Kreme. Of course. . . Ed's was just a few blocks away. . . .

She began to walk east in his direction. For chrissake, this was ridiculous. She could sneak in a little meeting with Ed. Just a few minutes. Maybe give him a slightly better explanation than the crap she'd been dishing out and despising herself for? Didn't he deserve that? Just like he'd said?

Or maybe they wouldn't even have to talk. She could

announce a no-talking rule, and they could just have a quick hug. Or maybe a little kiss. Or maybe even. . . Honestly, it was so late already, would they even be watching her that closely now? Whoever the hell *they* were? Would it really make that much of a difference if she stayed the night? One extra night? *God,* she wanted to stay the night. She wanted that so badly, it was sending painful bolts of electricity down her spine. . . .

Okay, STOP. No, I mean literally STOP. Stop walking down this block.

She froze on Sixth between First and Second in front of a long row of Indian restaurants that had closed for the night.

Seeing Ed would only be for *her.* The hug, or the kiss, or. . . what she really wanted. . . would only be for her. And then Ed would be dead by the following day, and therefore so would she. It would not and could not happen. She wouldn't let it. In spite of the nuclear-powered, billion-gigawatt electromagnet that was pulling her toward his house and his arms and his bed. . . she would turn around now and thus extend his life for years to come.

Nope. Ed was home, but she couldn't go all the way home. Downtown was the closest she was going to get. Or maybe. . .

The park. At least she could revisit Washington Square Park tonight. There was a time when she had felt like that park was the only true home she had. It was too late to see Zolov or Renny or good old Mr. Haq. But at least the arch would always be lit up. Who knew? Maybe there would even be some legitimate criminals there tonight. Criminals she would be damn sure not to befriend or bring home as roommates.

HEATHER HAD GOTTEN COMPLETELY
lost in the world of Josh's lips. And his hands, and his incredibly muscular arms, and the dent that ran down the center of his chest that she could even feel through his shirt, and. . .

Yes, she was plastered, absolutely, but still. . . Josh had been right about Washington Square Park. Being wrapped up in his arms, straddling his legs, with his coat wrapped around her shoulders and his lips sending rich and glorious tingles through her entire body. The park at night did feel completely new. She and Josh had already created an entirely new memory for Heather, a whole new mental association with that park. Or in this case, more of a *physical* association, really. But it was a physical association that was, just as Josh had promised, unforgettable.

That was, until Josh quite suddenly jerked away

from Heather and lifted her back onto the side of the park bench.

"Wh-What's wrong?" Heather asked, trying to catch her breath as she did a quick mirrorless lipstick-smudge removal around the edges of her mouth.

"Nothing," Josh assured her. "God, not you, *definitely* not you." He shot out of his seat.

"Well, if not me, then *who?*"

"Oh, man." Josh sighed, backing away from the bench. "I am *so sorry*, Heather, I totally forgot. . . ."

"Forgot *what?*" Heather squawked in a state of pure, perhaps drunken confusion. "What did you forget at two in the morning?"

"It's. . ." Josh slapped his hands to his sides and sighed. "You know, it's so complicated, if I tried to explain it to you now, it would take forever."

"I *have* forever."

Josh's eyes darted out into the park and then to his watch. "Oh, damn hell damn hell. I'm so sorry, Heather, I've got to run. I'll call you first thing in the morning, okay? I had an amazing time tonight. *Amazing.*"

"It *is* first thing in the morning."

"*Second* thing, then," he said, backing toward the bushes that led toward MacDougal Street. "I'll call you second thing!"

And then he took off in a full sprint. Like a bat out of hell.

Heather was absolutely, unequivocally confounded.

Had she done something wrong? Was it something about her kisses? Had she *said* something wrong? No, that wasn't possible, given that neither one of them had said *anything* since they'd landed on that park bench together. What. . . the hell. . . was that about? How could he have just left her in the park alone that way?

"Heather!"

Heather looked out at the center of the park and saw a blurry figure sprinting toward her. It couldn't be Josh, since he'd just taken off in the other direction. Besides, it sounded like a woman's voice.

"Heather, wait there!" she hollered intensely.

Heather was indeed awfully drunk, and everything was awfully blurry, but it sure as hell looked a lot like. . .

"Gaia?"

FOR JUST A MOMENT, GAIA HONESTLY wished she hadn't seen him. She wished that she didn't possess nearly telescopic vision. Then she wouldn't have had to know it tonight. Then she wouldn't have had to confront Heather with it **Nonathletic Drunk** tonight. Then she could have had just one ever so brief *un*horrible moment to herself in her home away from home of Washington Square Park.

But she had seen him, and she knew it. Just as much as she knew that he had seen her and taken off into the bushes. And she had once made the mistake of not confronting Heather about potential grave danger. It was outside this very park that she'd made that mistake. And she had promised herself that she would never make that mistake again.

The question of why wasn't important now. That would surely present itself down the line. Right now, the only priority was speed. More speed. More speed to catch up with him. More speed to put an end to *whatever* kind of insane scheme this was, right now.

She stomped right up to the edge of the pavement just before the bushes, where Heather was sitting in an utterly dumbfounded state.

"Gaia?"

"Wait here," Gaia ordered as she leaped into the bushes, breaking through branches and twigs, scanning her entire field of vision with robotic precision. "Josh?" she screamed out viciously. "Jesus, you freakin' *baby!*" she hollered, her lungs filling up with the overwhelming purified hatred she had for him. "Running into the goddamn bushes? Are you kidding me? What is this, fourth grade? Olly, olly, oxen-free, you son of a bitch! Come out, come out, wherever you are."

She came out of the bushes right to the edge of the park on MacDougal, and that was that. He'd made it out. Somehow. "Son of a bitch!" she hollered.

She quickly turned around, crashing back through the bushes and back to Heather, who was in the exact same position as when she'd last seen her. Utterly bewildered and perhaps. . . a little dizzy? She seemed to be swaying a bit from side to side as she suffered through what appeared to be her very intense confusion.

Gaia dropped down next to Heather on the park bench and twisted her body enough to put them face-to-face. "Heather, are you okay?"

"What are you doing here?" asked Heather with a catch in her voice, as she continuously looked back behind her into the bushes. It was clear that she considered Gaia's presence an intrusion.

But Gaia didn't care. She wasn't going to waste any time on this one. She wasn't going to be gentle about it or take Heather through it slowly, because Heather had to be one hundred percent crystal clear that this scam had to stop *now,* as in this minute, this hour.

"Okay, Heather, I need you to listen to me, all right? I need you to listen to what I tell you and then *believe* me. It's very important that you believe me because this is *not* bullshit, okay? I am *not* bullshitting you. That guy you were just with. . . Josh. . ."

"Yeah. . . ?"

"I *know* that guy, and he is *bad news.* He works for

some horrible people, and he's trying to set up some kind of trap with you. I don't know what yet, but I won't have to know if you just take my. . . no, it's more than advice. You can't see him, Heather. You can't see him ever again, do you understand? You've got to call that thing off as of today. As of right now."

Heather narrowed her eyes at Gaia as if Gaia had just delivered a speech in Portuguese. "Wait. . . *what* are you talking about?"

Gaia slammed her hands down on her lap and rolled her eyes heavenward. If Heather was drunk, then this was the worst possible time to have this conversation. But it wasn't the kind of conversation that could be had tomorrow after she and Josh had gone out for a little lunch or something. The rules had to be established right now, and Gaia was willing to say anything necessary to set those rules. Including more of the truth.

"I'm talking about your *date*, Heather, or your boyfriend or whatever he is. You cannot trust him. He is plotting something against you, and against me, and even maybe against Ed—I have no idea. You have to *stop* seeing him. Do you understand?"

Heather rolled her eyes and began to fit her feet back into her shoes, which were on the ground. "Gaia, are you aware that you sound completely crazy right now?" She shoved the second shoe on and got slowly to her feet.

Gaia got up with her, not wanting to lose eye contact on this particular issue. *Keep trying, Gaia. Try another approach.* "Heather, please, I don't want to make the same mistake with you twice. Think about this. . . If I had told you that night that there was a slasher in the park, would you have believed me?"

"Of course, I would have," Heather snapped, giving her an evil glare.

"Well, then, will you believe me now when I tell you. . . that guy you were just here with on this bench. . . is a murderer."

"What?" Heather squawked. "Okay, you know what, Gaia? I think that's enough. I think I know what you're doing, and if you stop now, then maybe I'll just forget about this, okay? Now, I've had a little bit to drink tonight, and my boyfriend just went to bed, so if you don't mind, I think I'd like to go to bed as well." Heather took a few stumbling practice steps before she removed her shoes again and began walking more quickly.

Of course, Gaia knew that the odds of getting through to Heather were practically nil, but she had no choice other than to try. "Heather, wait, please, just hear me out for one second. *One second.*"

Heather finally stopped and turned back to Gaia. "What?" She sighed dubiously.

"Look," Gaia said, looking her as sincerely in the eye as she knew how or had ever done before. "I'm going to tell you this only because I don't know how else to convince you of the kind of trouble you're in. And this isn't how I would have wanted to tell you at all, but Heather. . . that man. . . Josh. He killed Sam, Heather. Sam is dead."

Heather went completely silent as she stared into Gaia's eyes. Her hands slowly drifted up from her sides to her hips as she leaned her face closer to Gaia's. "You. . . are. . . unbelievable."

"What are you talking about?"

"You know, I tried to give you the benefit of the doubt," Heather said, her voice beginning to simmer with a very angry kind of manic energy. "And this is what I get?"

"What—"

"I see what you're doing, Gaia," Heather announced, shooting more and more anger through her eyes. "I just never thought you had it in you to stoop so low as that kind of a sick lie about Sam. I mean, what the hell is wrong with you? Is it really *that* important to you to ruin any relationship I have?"

"Heather, don't be ridic—"

"Any relationship, Gaia! *Any relationship!*" Something in Heather had just snapped, and Gaia could see it in her eyes. "I mean, it's uncanny! I love Sam, you take Sam. I love Ed, you take Ed. Now I love Josh, you get *one glimpse* of him and you're jealous already! I mean, do you have any idea how sick that is? Are you just clinically jealous of me twenty-four hours a day? Have you seen a shrink about this? Because you really should, Gaia. And you should tell him that you actually have a sick enough mind to tell me not just that Sam is *dead*, but that *Josh* killed him, just so you can keep me away from *both of them*? Killing two birds with one disgusting lie? What is that, Gaia? What the hell *is* that?"

Gaia wanted to get one word in somehow. One word of sanity amidst Heather's attack of total drunken insanity, but barring a slap in the face, the opportunity simply wasn't there. "Heather—"

"You know, for a *second* there, I actually thought that we were becoming *friends*. How utterly idiotic of me was that?"

"We were bec—"

"Now I see that you're the *exact same*. You're the exact same person you were when you first came to this school. You're just evil and conniving and jealous and sick in the freaking head! You'd say *anything* to take a man away from me. Anything! You're a jealous, man-eating *bitch*, Gaia, and I just want you to do me one favor. I want you to stay the hell away from me. And stay the hell away from Josh."

Heather grabbed her shoes and took off at a sur-prisingly fast sprint, for a nonathletic drunk in stocking feet.

Gaia stood in the middle of the park at a complete loss. All she could think of was the fact that she hadn't been called a bitch this many times in one day since...

What the hell was she thinking? She'd never been called a bitch this many times in one day. That was what made today... so very special.

From: gaia13@alloymail.com
To: omoore@alloymail.com
Time: 2:45 A.M.
Re: Answers

Oliver,

I have no idea if this e-mail address is even operable anymore, but that's how pathetically desperate I have become.

I have been left with no choice but to contact you. I require some answers to a vast number of questions, and I have lost what little remaining support system I had.

If I thought there was any chance of another source being able to provide answers, believe me, I would not have contacted you. But you see, there are simply no remaining figures in my life whom I can trust.

So, sadly, I might as well try you.

Please respond.

From: omoore@alloymail.com
To: gaia13@alloymail.com
Time: 3:02 A.M.
Re: Answers

Dearest Gaia,

   I am thrilled to hear from you and want so
much to speak with you and make up for our last
most unexpected and horrid good-bye.

   I am currently out of the country, but upon my
return, I will be happy to answer any and all of
your questions with as much detail as I can and
with complete honesty. Fear not, Gaia. You won't
be alone for much longer.

   I thank you for putting your trust in me, however tenuous it may be. Looking forward to our
meeting.

                            Love,
                            Uncle Oliver

Wrong about Heather. Wrong about Gen. Wrong about Tatiana. My track record here is beyond pathetic. God, what if I've made the wrong choice about Ed, too? Maybe avoiding him is the worst possible choice I could make? I mean, what has happened to me here? Is *this* what fear is? Just buckets and buckets of horrible judgment? No instincts at all. I honestly thought that being fear-*less* was ruining my instincts, but maybe it's the other way around?

Listen to me. Just *listen* to me. I'm not *me*. I'm not Gaia. I'm just this lost, amorphous blob of a human being with a bunch of unanswerable questions. I came downtown to try and find some stitch of home, just the faintest reminder of who I am, and all I've ended up with is *more* stupid questions. I mean, there has to be a limit, doesn't there? There has to be a limit to the amount of unanswerable questions I can live with.

Or let me rephrase, *not* in the form of a question. Let me at least speak like Gaia even if I can't be her:

I have reached my limit of unanswerable questions.

I mean, for chrissake, I thought I had surrendered already, but apparently not. Apparently I need to surrender to my surrender. Because I need answers now. I need to know who I can trust. I need to know if I'm going to be stuck with these nagging fear symptoms for the rest of my nonlife. I need to know what on earth Josh is up to with Heather. Does Loki have it in for her? And most of all, I need to know if I'm protecting Ed from someone or just shooting myself in the foot with a giant loneliness gun.

Do you know what's even more tragic? I haven't just left myself with a hill of insurmountable questions. I've left myself with no one to answer them. No one except that vulture who

always seems to be circling whenever I'm dead in the water.

   So be it. I'll complete my
transition into the penultimate
loser and reopen that line of
communication. Because it's the
only one I have. Yes, I'm giving
up *again*. I do hereby surrender
from my surrender. Or to be more
specific. . . I'm saying "uncle."

F E A R L E S S

. . . a girl born without the fear gene

I'm supposed to be a genius.

I'm supposed to be able to

see things other people can't.

It's kind of ironic.

Because I can't see the truth.

Even when it's right in front of me.

the mediator

A new school, annoying step-brothers and disastrous first dates – these are nothing in comparison to Susannah's other problems. The ghostly hunk sitting in her new bedroom and the psycho spirit haunting the locker room who's out for revenge on her ex-boyfriend – that's what Susannah calls real trouble . . .